Daniel stood in the bow of the boat, practicing his blocking exercises.

"When am I going to learn to punch?" he asked.

In response, Mr. Miyagi began to rock the boat, breaking Daniel's rhythm and tipping him. Unceremoniously, Daniel landed, shoulder first, in the cold water. When he emerged, sputtering, Mr. Miyagi answered his question.

"When learn keep dry," he said wryly, and helped Daniel climb back into the boat.

"More important than learn punch or block," he continued, handing Daniel a towel, "is to learn balance. Balance is key. When balance good, karate good. Everything good. When balance bad, better fix quick or pack up and go home. Understand?"

"Yeah."

The
Karate
Kid

COLUMBIA PICTURES Presents

A JERRY WEINTRAUB Production of A JOHN G. AVILDSEN Film

"THE KARATE KID"

Starring RALPH MACCHIO · NORIYUKI "PAT" MORITA · ELISABETH SHUE

Music by BILL CONTI · Director of Photography R.J. LOUIS · Written by ROBERT MARK KAMEN

Produced by JERRY WEINTRAUB · Directed by JOHN G. AVILDSEN

The Karate Kid

Novelization by B.B. Hiller
Based on the screenplay by Robert Mark Kamen

SCHOLASTIC INC.
New York Toronto London Auckland Sydney

ISBN 0-590-43524-8

12 11 10 9 8 7 6 5 4 3 2   2 3/9

Printed in the U.S.A.   01

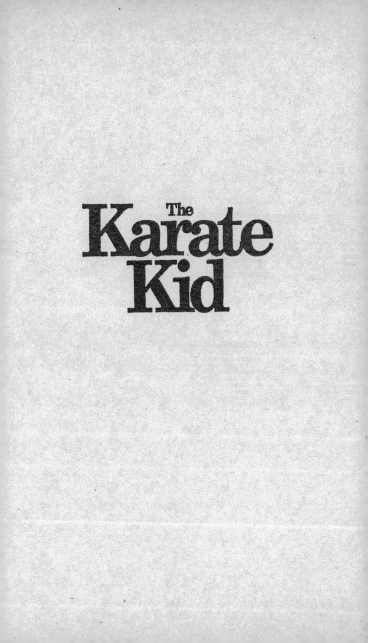

The Karate Kid

Chapter
One

THE ancient, overloaded Chevy station wagon lumbered through the streets.

Daniel looked out the car window to inspect his new hometown, Reseda, California. It didn't look like Newark. In fact, nothing about California reminded Daniel of New Jersey. He wondered how long it would be before Reseda became familiar — before these streets became his.

He tried to convince himself that Reseda was special. Everything here would be special. He was leaving the ordinary behind. After all, he thought, anything could happen in California.

His thoughts were interrupted by the nervous chatter of his mother, Lucille.

"Just imagine, Danny — a pool! Our new apartment building has a swimming pool!"

"Yeah, Mom," he said to her. "You told me about that already, and about the palm trees, too." He was skeptical. Every new home he'd ever had was supposed to be better than the one before it. He couldn't remember one that actually had been.

" 'South Seas Apartments' — doesn't that sound romantic? The rental agent said it was 'charming.' "

"Mom," Danny said evenly. "You know that 'charming' really means 'small and run-down.' " Suddenly even California began to seem ordinary. He didn't like that.

"Okay, first a left, then a right after the school — I wonder if that will be your school — then two more blocks, and on the right . . ."

Daniel's eyes followed the instructions.

"Look at that, Dan! Would you look?!"

The paint was blistered and peeling on the pink stucco arch that proclaimed SOUTH SEAS APARTMENTS. They drove through the entry way and came to a stop at the building entrance. Slowly, Daniel climbed out of the car and began unpacking their things from the car's roof. First to come off was his own bicycle.

"Hey, Dan, isn't this great?" Lucille pointed upwards. "Know what *that* means?"

Reluctantly, his eyes flicked up to view four tall, unkempt palm trees by the doorway.

"Yeah," he answered. "Besides earthquakes, I've got to watch out for falling coconuts now."

"Wise guy. I'll tell you what it means: No more Newark winters."

It wasn't so much that California was bad,

just that it was different. His enthusiasm couldn't match his mother's.

"I like winters," he protested.

"You like sore throats? You like frozen toes?"

"I don't like smog."

Undaunted, Lucille continued. "How about swimming? You like that, right? Did I tell you about the pool here?"

"Yeah, a hundred times."

"So, make it a hundred and one. Open your eyes, my darling son, this is our Garden of Eden."

Daniel tried to believe it.

"— and we're in apartment 2D." With that, Lucille picked up two suitcases and headed for their apartment. Daniel watched her leave, then balanced a box of pots and pans on the handles of his bicycle, and after a bit of a struggle, followed her. When he got to the courtyard door, he realized he could not free a hand to open it. His feet, however, were available for the job.

"Kiaaiiiii!" he cried, as his left foot crashed the door open. From the other side came a thud and an indignant:

"What the —!"

Daniel entered the hallway and found a boy his own age picking himself up off the floor and rubbing his arm. Apparently, this was the victim of Daniel's karate kick.

"Oh, sorry."

"That's okay. I guess I should have looked. You the new people in 2D?"

"Yeah."

"Freddy Fernandez, 1A."

"Daniel LaRusso. Glad to meet you."

"Here, let me help you," offered Freddy. Daniel accepted gladly as Freddy took the pots and pans and led the way across the courtyard.

"Where are you from?"

"New Jersey."

"Wow! What are you doing here?"

"My mom got a great job with a company out here. Rocket Computers." He thought of the brochure they'd sent and mimicked the motto, "Flight to the Future!"

"Never heard of it," said Freddy.

"It's up and coming," Daniel explained, and then realized he'd made a pun. They both laughed.

As they turned a corner, the pool came into view. Daniel's worst expectations were realized. It was small, half empty, and had an unhealthy green hue. A deflated rubber swan floated listlessly in the murky liquid. Daniel hoped his mother had not noticed the pool. He was afraid she would be disappointed, and she'd had such high hopes for it.

Next to the pool sat an old woman doing a crossword puzzle. Beside her was a scruffy dog, panting in the August heat.

"Hi ya, pup," said Daniel, scratching the dog's ear. In response, the dog thumped his tail wearily on the cracked concrete. The old woman scrutinized Daniel for a moment.

"This place is a dump. You should go back to New Jersey."

"How do you know I'm from New Jersey?"

"Because I'm from New Jersey. I've got a nose for my own kind."

"Oh yeah? Where you from in New Jersey?" Daniel challenged her.

"Parsippany. And I never should have left."

"My Uncle Louie is from Parsippany."

Interested, the woman said, "Louie Fontini?"

"Louie LaRusso."

"Never heard of him," she declared, turning back to her crossword puzzle.

Freddy and Daniel continued to Daniel's apartment.

"She's missing a few screws," Freddy explained.

"She's all right." Daniel defended her. He had a nose for *his* own kind, too.

"Hey," said Freddy. "When you came through that door back there, you kicked it pretty hard. Was that karate? Do you know karate?"

"Uh, yeah." Daniel thought of the dingy gym at the Y where he'd had eight karate classes. Freddy was so impressed that it didn't seem likely he knew anything about karate. A little knowledge could carry Danny a long way. So Daniel thought.

"Been doing it long?" asked Freddy.

"A while," he responded, evasively.

"Ever use it?"

Daniel remembered the door he'd just opened.

"Sure. A couple of times."

"Bet you can really kick some butts, huh?"

Daniel shrugged modestly.

"I'd like to learn some of that. Maybe you could teach me sometime, huh?"

Daniel nodded.

They came to the door marked 2D. Freddy balanced the carton of pots and pans on Daniel's bicycle handlebars again and asked what he had planned for the next day.

"Nothing."

"We're having a party — some kids from our school — at the beach tomorrow. Sort of adios to summer since school starts the day after. Want to come, too?"

"Sure."

"Great. I'll come get you in the morning." Freddy turned and left.

As Daniel opened the door, he began feeling optimistic. Maybe this really would be a special place. Adios Newark. Hello California.

Chapter
Two

"NOT a word about the pool, please," Daniel's mother said as he stepped into the apartment, looking for a place to park his bike and put the pots and pans. "I'll call the apartment manager first thing in the morning to fix it," she continued. "I promise you, we *will* have a pool —"

"That's okay, Mom." Daniel reassured her. "Say, did you tell that lady downstairs where we were from?"

"Yeah. Doesn't she remind you of Aunt Tessy?"

"More like Uncle Louie," said Daniel, unpacking kitchen utensils. "Remember that mangy dog of his — what was his name? Old Ben? He always stayed near Uncle Louie."

"Sure," she said. "You know, I really think we're going to like it here. I never felt so positive about anything in my life. This was really the right move. I'm telling you, Dan. This is it!"

Daniel nodded and reached for the faucet. As he turned on the water, it sprayed all over him.

"Oh!" said his mother. "The faucet's broken!" She began to dry him off, flicking at the water with a sweater she had been holding. "The real estate woman told me that there's a handyman around here. See if you can find him, okay?"

"Sure," said Daniel, holding a half-filled bowl of water.

"What's that for?"

"Uncle Louie's dog." Daniel paused at the door. "I got invited to a party tomorrow."

"Hey, great. You see? I told you this was going to be our Garden of Eden!"

"But I was going to help you unpack."

"I don't remember saying anything about that."

Daniel smiled. "I must have had you confused with another mother of mine. Thanks, Mom."

A few minutes later, Daniel put the bowl in front of the dog by the pool. Eagerly, the dog lapped at the water.

"How's that, Old Ben?" The dog stopped drinking long enough to lick Daniel's face. The woman was not as friendly.

"I hope you take my advice and go back to New Jersey."

"We're discussing it. Where can I find the handyman?"

"You go down there and you take a right, where it goes to the left, but not too far right, then you go left and his room is on the right."

"Left then right?"

"No, right where it's left, then left, then to the right."

"Sure," said Daniel, lost already. Somehow, though, he found the door marked MAINTENANCE. He entered.

It was unlike anything he had expected. The large room was spotlessly clean and meticulously tidy. There was no evidence of any handyman's tools, though Daniel supposed they could be in the cabinets on the walls. A large bookcase by the window near the door held dozens of miniature trees. Daniel recognized them from pictures. They were bonsai trees — a specialty of Japanese gardening.

Beyond the shelf, Daniel could hear a snapping sound. He followed his ears and was startled to find himself looking at an old Oriental man. Daniel stepped back and took in the scene. The man must have been seventy years old. He was wearing blue coveralls and was brandishing a pair of chopsticks. The man—whose name was Miyagi according to his name patch — appeared to be trying to catch a fly with the chopsticks.

Snap!

Daniel found his voice.

"Are you the maintenance man?"

"Hai."

"Hello. Are you the maintenance man?"

"Hai."

"Hi, to you. Are you —" Then Daniel remembered that "hai" is Japanese for "yes."

"Oh, we're the new people in 2D."

A fly's buzzing held the old man's attention. His body was absolutely still. His eyes followed the noise — the only movement in his serene face.

"Uh, our faucet's broken."

The man's attention was rivetted to the fly. He did not seem to have heard Daniel. Daniel tried again.

"Can you come fix it?"

"Hai."

Daniel watched, perplexed. Suddenly, the man's arm shot out.

Snap!

The arm was withdrawn. The fly continued to buzz. The eyes continued to follow the noise.

"Um, can I tell my mom when?"

"When what?" Mr. Miyagi asked evenly, still holding his body frozen.

"When you'll come to fix the faucet."

"After," he answered.

"After what?"

"After."

That, it seemed, was as much information as Daniel was going to get from that strange man — the handyman with no tools. What kind of man, thought Daniel, would try to catch a fly with chopsticks? What kind of man *could* catch a fly with chopsticks?

Chapter
Three

THE next day, Daniel found himself on a small strip of secluded beach at the foot of a hill. Freddy introduced him to his friends, Allan, Chuck, and Billy. The five of them played soccer with a ball Daniel had brought. Another dozen or so kids were there, too, swimming, sunning, and picnicking. It was a California beach party just the way they looked on TV, Daniel thought. Only this one was real.

Daniel was glad he had brought the soccer ball. Soccer was a sport he was really good at — much better than his new friends were — so it was a chance to show off.

Freddy kicked the ball to Daniel, but it was way out of control — high over his head. Daniel turned to watch as the ball lobbed onto a blanket where a group of girls were sitting around a radio, giggling and talking. He jogged over to retrieve it.

There, sitting on the blanket, was the most gorgeous girl Daniel had ever seen in all of his fifteen-and-a-half years. She was a California girl — smooth blond hair, blue eyes, ski jump nose — and had a lot of curves in all the right places. Her white bikini showed off a summer's worth of beautiful tan.

Daniel was dumbstruck. The girl, aware of his interest, caught his eye and smiled. A grin broke out on Daniel's face. He took the soccer ball she offered him and did the only thing he could think of. He bounced it on his knee, to the other knee, to his head, to his instep, then up to his hand. Joe Cool.

The girl's eyes twinkled. All those hours of practice were worth it, thought Daniel. She *was* impressed. She rose from the blanket and ran with her friends toward the water. Daniel followed her with his eyes. Before diving into the surf, she gave Daniel one more look over her shoulder and winked.

His knees felt weak.

"Who's that?" he asked Freddy.

"The Hills."

"What's the Hills?"

"Encino Hills and it means rich. Here, show us some of that hot dog stuff you were doing for Ali."

Somewhat reluctantly, Daniel stopped staring at the swimmers and joined his new friends.

Soon, the afternoon turned to evening. The fog rolled in and the picnickers gathered around campfires. The boys were talking about the girls. Freddy was impressed with Daniel's apparent magnetism for Ali.

"Hey, man, she's hot for you."

Daniel was dubious.

"Yeah, sure."

"Make a move," Freddy dared him. Daniel shrugged. He didn't want to make a monkey of himself in front of that girl. Allan taunted him.

"Maybe they ain't got no moves where he comes from. Maybe they never make moves in New Jersey."

Daniel took the bait.

"I've got moves you turkeys never heard of."

Mischievously, Freddy lofted the soccer ball back over to Ali's blanket.

"Let's see," said Freddy.

Hesitantly, Daniel rose to the challenge, but Ali made it easy for him. She stood up as he approached and handed him the ball.

"Let me see you do that stuff again."

Relieved, he repeated his flawless performance of the afternoon.

"Is that hard to learn?"

"Not really," he said modestly.

"Can you show me how to do it?"

"Sure," he said gallantly.

A few minutes later, one of Ali's friends ran over to them.

"Hey, Ali," she called. "There's Johnny with the Cobras." She pointed to the hill, where Daniel saw a group of boys on dirt bikes, watching the picnickers on the beach.

Ali shrugged and returned her attention to Daniel and the soccer ball. She tried bouncing the ball from knee to knee and was actually pretty good at it. Daniel just enjoyed watching her move. She was something. She was even pretty good with a soccer ball.

Then came the sound of dirt bikes descending the hill. Ali seemed to pale as the sound came closer. Daniel had no idea what was going on, but he knew he didn't like it. Unexpectedly, Ali tossed the soccer ball so it was caught by the wind and carried down to the water's edge. Obligingly, Daniel chased it for her.

Once he'd captured the ball, he walked back toward Ali, but saw her deep in conversation with one of the boys from the dirt bike gang. Daniel was disappointed, but he didn't want to interfere, so he walked back toward Freddy's group.

Suddenly, Ali's radio blared so loudly that everyone turned. They saw Johnny trying to yell over the sound and then watched as he turned off the radio.

"I don't *want* to talk," said Ali, defiantly. And she turned the radio back on. Johnny grabbed it from her and threw it into the sand near Daniel who went to pick it up.

"Don't touch it!" yelled Johnny. Daniel picked it up anyway.

"You deaf?" Johnny ripped the radio from Daniel's hands.

Daniel wasn't sure what was going on

except that he could tell Johnny was about to explode. He hoped it wouldn't be at Ali.

"Come on, man," Daniel said in a voice he hoped would calm.

Johnny held out the radio to Daniel. "You want it?" he asked menacingly. Then, suddenly, he rammed the radio at Daniel, knocking him down.

Daniel's own rage erupted and he sprang at Johnny. Johnny deftly stepped aside and Daniel tripped into the sand.

"Stop it!" cried Ali, in vain.

Once again, Daniel charged at Johnny, but this time Johnny didn't step aside. As Daniel neared him, Johnny's leg shot out and caught him in the chest, throwing him to the ground and knocking the wind out of him.

All the kids on the beach gathered around Johnny and Daniel.

"Get up," they yelled at Daniel. Slowly, he pulled himself up, shaking his head to clear his vision.

"How about it, hero," jeered Johnny. "Had enough?"

For a second Daniel didn't move. Then, without warning, he lunged at Johnny, swinging wildly as he came. One of his punches connected with Johnny's nose, and a small trickle of blood appeared. Johnny stepped back, surprised.

"Now we're even, right?" Daniel said hopefully.

Johnny stared at Daniel. As their eyes measured each other, Johnny's body moved, catlike, into a karate stance, knees flexed, arms raised, one to defend, one to attack.

"No mercy," said Johnny.

"Stop it!" Ali tried again.

"You started it, Ali," said Johnny. "Now I have to finish it. All *I* wanted to do was talk." His voice was cold.

"No mercy!" chanted Johnny's friends.

Daniel's dwindling cheering section was Freddy.

"Karate him!" he called. "Drop him now!"

It was over in a few seconds. Johnny's lightning speed karate kicks downed Daniel and he could barely stumble to his feet. Johnny and his gang mounted their dirt bikes and rode away.

Soon, a trail of dust was all that was left of them. Except the pain.

Chuck turned to Freddy with disgust.

"You sure pick cool people to be friends with."

"Hey, man," said Freddy. "Gimme a break! He told me he knew karate."

They turned and left the beach.

Ali came up to Daniel.

"Are you okay?"

"Leave me alone."

"Let me help you," she said kindly. But Daniel didn't want kindness. He'd been humiliated and that hurt in a place kindness couldn't reach.

"I just want to be alone."

And he was. Daniel had never been so alone in his life.

Chapter
Four

THE oversized aviator's reflecting sunglasses did the trick. They completely covered Daniel's black eye. He checked in the mirror one more time. Satisfied, he walked into the kitchen for breakfast.

His mother was busy at the stove. She heard Daniel walk in and turned to him, "Oh! Now don't *we* look California!"

"Yeah."

"How was the party?"

"Okay."

"Just 'okay'? It must have been more than 'okay.' I didn't hear you come in. Any friend material?"

Hastily, Daniel poured himself a glass of orange juice and answered, "Some. I've got to go."

"Eat first."

"Thanks, but I'm not hungry."

"I didn't ask if you were hungry. You'll

need the get-up-and-go you get from a good breakfast so you can be charming and wow those Valley Girls on your first day of school."

"Sure. See you, Mom." Daniel headed for the door, but he hadn't fooled her.

"Daniel," she said. "Take off the glasses."

"Why?"

"Because I asked you to."

"Hey, Mom, it's the California look," he tried.

"Take 'em off. I want to see those baby brown eyes."

"Mom," he protested.

"Now!" His mother slammed her hand on the counter. The plates danced with her anger. Slowly, Daniel removed the glasses to reveal his eye, swollen and purple.

"Oh, Daniel! What happened?"

Daniel wanted to tell her something she could believe. She had enough worries of her own and he didn't want her to have to worry about him, too.

"I hit a curb with my bike, then the curb hit me. I guess it was really mad, huh?" he joked, feebly.

"Can you see okay? Do you want to stay home?"

"It looks lots worse than it feels, really, Mom. Don't worry. Now I've got to get to school." He kissed her on the cheek gingerly, put his glasses back on, and walked to the door.

"It's okay, really, Mom." The last thing he

saw as he walked out was his mother's worried face.

The first day of school was a maze of loneliness for Daniel. Everybody seemed to belong there except him. Several times he was sure people were talking about him, but it seemed impossible that he was already the talk of the school. Daniel tried to concentrate on his schedule, the school map, and his teachers' names. The only thing he really wanted to do was get to soccer tryouts. He needed to do something he was really good at.

At two-thirty, he changed into his gym shorts, jogged to the soccer field, and began dribbling the soccer ball along with fifty other hopefuls for the soccer team.

"Hey, Karate Kid!"

Daniel turned to see Freddy and Chuck jogging around the field.

"Let's see them moves!" taunted Freddy.

Chuck smirked, "The only move *he* knows is how to get beat, right, Karate Kid? You want him to teach you how to lose, Freddy?"

"Nah, I already know that one."

Daniel closed his ears to the comments and concentrated on his dribbling until one of the cheerleaders came and tapped him on the shoulder. It was Ali.

He turned in surprise and smiled, but as he turned, she saw his eye and her face fell.

"Don't worry," he reassured her. "It looks worse than it feels."

"I hope so. It looks terrible," she said as

she examined it more closely. Daniel was pleased by her attention. "Listen," she continued, "I never got a chance to thank you."

"It was nothing. Sorry about the radio."

"You should have let the dope have it. I'm more sorry about your eye."

"But it wasn't his radio."

"You're right. It wasn't," said Ali, admiring Daniel's chivalry. Daniel's knees began to go weak again. He wondered what it was about this girl that made him melt — and say dumb things.

"Now, isn't that something?" he said.

"What?"

"We think alike. We agree that it wasn't his radio."

Ali glowed, happily.

"Want to see something else we do alike? Watch this," she said.

Ali picked up the soccer ball. She bounced it on her knee, to her other knee, to her head, and almost to her instep. Daniel caught the ball for her before it went out of control.

"Well, almost alike," she said, blushing.

"That's terrif —" but Daniel was interrupted by an insistent whistle and an officious cry.

"Cheerleaders! Over here! Now!"

"I've got to go."

"Hey, what's your name?" Ali stopped and turned.

"Ali Mills. Ali with an 'i.'" She smiled at him one more time and rushed off, almost bumping into Johnny. Daniel realized that

Johnny had witnessed his entire conversation with Ali.

The soccer coach's whistle brought Daniel to attention. He listened to the instructions and found himself passing the ball back and forth with a boy he didn't know. He concentrated on his technique, which was, in fact, very good, and he quickly gained the respect of the boy he was paired with. The coach watched for a while, then moved on to the others. In the background, Daniel was vaguely aware of the cheerleaders' practice. Once or twice, he glanced over to watch Ali-with-an-i.

The coach cut them into practice teams and then Daniel had the opportunity he'd wanted. He got the ball and began a strong drive downfield with it. Ducking to the right, faking to the left, he found himself in the clear with an open shot on the goal — except for one person: Johnny's henchman, Bobby.

Daniel faked to the left and Bobby followed him, realizing too late it was a fake. As Daniel switched to the right evading him, Bobby slid onto the turf and hooked Daniel's leg from behind with his spiked shoes, downing Daniel and wrenching his knee. Daniel winced in pain before pulling himself up. When he stood, he saw Bobby, grinning. Behind Bobby, on the sidelines, Johnny and Tommy were nodding their approval.

No one else had seen what happened. Furious, Daniel sprang at Bobby and wrestled him down to the ground. Whistles began to blow and coaches appeared from all over the field, pulling the boys apart.

The soccer coach looked at Daniel sternly.

"You! Out!"

"But, coach, he hooked me, deliberately," protested Daniel.

"I said out. There's no room for fighting on this team." Then the coach turned to the rest of the boys. "Now, back to it!"

Dejected, Daniel limped off the field past the grinning Cobras and past the cheerleaders. As he walked into the field house, the last thing he heard was the cheerleading squad: "Fight, team, fight!"

Yeah, he thought. Fight, team.

Chapter
Five

DANIEL practiced his smile again.

It wasn't easy. He didn't have much to smile about as he thought over the events of the last two days. But his mother was determined to make their new home succeed. Daniel didn't want to be the one to ruin it for her. Maybe she was right, he thought, wryly. Maybe the best thing about this Garden of Eden *was* that swimming pool.

The front door opened. Daniel pasted the well-practiced smile on his face and greeted his mother easily.

"Hi, hon! How's the eye?" she asked, dashing in.

"Okay. What's the rush?"

"I got a job!"

"Yeah, I know. Rocket Computers. *Flight to the Future!*"

" 'Crashed in the Present' is more like it.

The company went bankrupt last Friday. Can you believe it? Isn't that my luck?"

"So, we're going home?"

"Honey, we *are* home. This is it." She walked into her bedroom, then came back out again. "Seen my black shoes?"

Daniel reached under the couch, found them, and handed them to her.

"So, what's this job?"

"It's just fantastic, honey. Listen to this story. I walked out of the former Rocket Computer offices, feeling pretty low — as you can imagine — and a woman comes flying out of this restaurant, The Orient Express — isn't that cute? — yelling about how she's going to quit. Right behind her, a guy is yelling, 'You can't quit. You're fired!' It's one minute to noon, people are coming in for lunch, and I'm the Number One applicant. I got the job. What a story, huh?"

Daniel couldn't hide his disappointment.

"So after going to school — all those night classes about computers — you're going to be a waitress?"

"Hostess, if you please."

"Big difference."

"Yes, Daniel, there is. But it's only temporary anyway. It'll feed us until something better comes along."

Daniel wanted to change the subject. He did have some good news, after all.

"I started driver's ed at school. I got my learner's permit."

"That's nice," his mother said, distracted.

She held up a pair of earrings to her lobes. "Do these go?"

"Sure. Listen, if I get enough practice in, I can get my license on my birthday."

"How do I look?"

Daniel pasted the smile back on his face. This time, however, the insincerity showed through.

"Great," he said, dully.

"Hon, there's stuff in the fridge for dinner. See you later." With that, she hurriedly pecked Daniel on the cheek and dashed out the door. He retreated to the corner of the sofa and his not-so-happy thoughts about the Garden of Eden. The door opened again. His mother stuck her head in and said, "How's Friday afternoon?"

"For what?"

"Driving lessons." Daniel beamed at his mother and then watched her leave.

After dinner, Daniel took out his karate book. He was glad he'd brought it from Newark. He thought that perhaps if he followed a careful regimen, he could get as good at karate as Johnny and then feed him some of his own medicine.

However, it didn't take long to figure out that the few lessons back in Newark and the book could not replace experience with a really good teacher. The movements and strategies simply could not be conveyed in a book. Well, it was all he had and it *was* better than nothing.

For perhaps the twenty-fifth time, Daniel

wondered why he had ever told Freddy he knew karate. Now he'd have to learn it for real to get back Freddy's friendship and to get back his own self-respect.

With renewed determination, he turned to his book. Carefully, he read the section on front snap kicks. He found that if he held the wall with one hand and the book with the other, he could read and follow the instructions. Somehow, though, it lacked Bruce Lee's fluid movement. Daniel persisted, setting a goal for himself of one hundred kicks, each side.

As he got to fifty-seven, there was a knock at the door. When he opened it, there was the handyman, Mr. Miyagi, holding a wrench and bowing.

"I come to fix faucet."

Daniel let him enter and then returned to his front snap kicks. From the sink, Mr. Miyagi watched.

"You study karate?" he asked.

"Yeah," answered Daniel, unbalanced.

"Oh, very good. Learn from book?"

"Sure, and a few months of lessons at the YMCA in Newark."

Mr. Miyagi turned back to the faucet. Daniel tried to continue his regimen. He switched from one leg to the other. He was even more awkward with that one. From the kitchen, Mr. Miyagi asked, "What happened to eye?"

"I fell off my bike." Mr. Miyagi came out

of the kitchen nodding that the faucet was fixed.

"And not hurt hands?" he asked. Daniel looked at his hands and then at the old man in amazement.

Funny that a stranger should notice it and not his mother. Daniel thought he was beginning to know how **a** fly might feel, pinioned between chopsticks.

Chapter
Six

THE next day, Daniel made it all the way until lunch period without getting into a fight.

While waiting for his change at the cashier, he noticed Ali scooting through the lunch line, apparently forgetting about food just to catch up with him. Breathless, she arrived by his side and handed the cashier a coin for her milk.

"Hi."

"Hello, Ali-with-an-i. How are you doing?"

"I'm okay. So, how do you like the Valley so far?"

Daniel thought for a second.

"It's not dull," he said, truthfully.

"Was Newark dull?"

"How did you know I was from Newark?"

"I asked."

Daniel smiled, pleased at Ali's attention.

"You sitting with anyone, Ali?"

"You," she said, weaving through the crowd toward some empty seats. "Say, I'm sorry about the soccer tryouts."

"That's okay, but it wasn't your fault. Those are the breaks."

"Yeah, well, you remember the guy you had trouble with on the beach?"

Could he forget?

"You mean Karate King?"

Ali nodded. "He's my ex-boyfriend."

That piece of news felt like a front snap kick to the gut; it also explained a lot. Daniel realized that he might just be crazy to be interested in Ali even if his knees melted every time she smiled at him.

Daniel cocked his head as if to listen to the voice of reason.

"I know. I know. You're right," he said to thin air.

Ali looked at him strangely.

"What was that all about?"

"It's this little voice," Daniel explained. "It gives me advice."

"And — ?"

"And, it said I'm some kind of coconut to pursue this, uh, matter."

"Daniel, I said 'ex,' and I meant it. It's over."

"How over?"

"Weeks." Ali spotted two vacant seats and led the way to them.

Daniel mumbled to no one in particular, "Weeks. What's weeks? One? Two? Fifty-two? One-half?"

Ali put her milk on the table and sat down. Daniel pulled out a chair, but when he sat down, there was a sickening squish. Too late, he realized there was something on the chair. When he stood up, he found a mashed piece of blueberry pie all over the seat of his white pants.

"Ooooh — gross!" said a girl at the next table.

Daniel looked for the culprit and he didn't have to look far. At a nearby table, Johnny and his henchmen were congratulating one another. All around, the kids spotted Daniel's pants and began laughing.

Ali was angry.

"You jerk!" she cried to Johnny. Daniel wiped the thick blueberry mess off his pants and held it in his hands as he walked calmly to Johnny.

"Don't even think about it, worm."

Daniel hesitated for a moment. He had, after all, made it to lunch period without a fight.

Calmly, he smeared the gob of blueberry gunk on Johnny's shirt. Mayhem erupted.

Chapter
Seven

DANIEL stared at the steamed dumplings on the plate before him at The Orient Express. With a chill, he remembered the words he had heard shouted in cadence that afternoon at the karate school he had visited, the Cobra Kai Dojo:

"What do we study?"

"The Way of the Fist!"

"And what is that Way?"

"Strike first. Strike hard!"

That was the way of the karate school where Daniel had thought he might train.

He remembered the "sensei" — the teacher, John Kreese. He was a dangerous-looking man, with cold, piercing eyes — the sort of person who just *looked* like he'd strike first and strike hard.

The students followed Mr. Kreese with awesome precision in their solemn ritual practice. Daniel had watched from the visitor's gallery, waiting to speak to the sensei after class, hoping he could afford the lessons he wanted so badly.

Finally, Mr. Kreese had stopped and turned the class over to one of his students. "Mr. Lawrence, run them through the drill."

A black belt leapt from the line of students, snapping his heels and arms together smartly, coming to attention. He bowed crisply from the waist and Kreese bowed back, stepping aside as the black belt sprinted to take his place as instructor.

It was just as Daniel had stood to ask Mr. Kreese about the lessons that the black belt had turned to face the visitor's gallery, and Daniel felt his stomach sink.

Kreese's number one student was Johnny. He looked as menacing in a gi with a black belt as he did on a dirt bike with a black leather jacket. The thought of Johnny with a black belt sickened Daniel and he had fled from the dojo.

Now eating at The Orient Express, the memory of the afternoon took away his appetite. Maybe the fortune cookie would bring him some good news.

His mother beamed as she joined him at the table.

"Guess what? I'm going to be trained as a manager. Isn't that great?"

"Yeah."

"They have this program: two nights a week. As soon as a spot opens, I'm in. And the benefits — I'd never get them working in computers. They pay for *every*thing."

"Great," said Daniel. His mother realized something was wrong.

"What's the matter, Dan?"

"Nothing."

Tenderly, she moved closer to Daniel. She put her hand on his.

"Honey," she began. "You remember that time we went to the country for the summer and you thought you would hate it because you had no friends there? You remember what happened?"

"Yeah. I got poison ivy."

"Yes, but you ended up meeting Kevin and Ken who became your best friends in the world and the three of you didn't want to come home. You've got to give it a try, Daniel. It's not easy, but we're not quitters, you and me, are we?"

"I guess not," Daniel shrugged and smiled, wanly.

"And what's with the girl situation, huh? What about these Valley Girls?"

"They're okay."

"Just okay? To me, it looks like the whole world went blond. You got an eye for anybody?"

Daniel shrugged again, but the beginnings of a smile around the corners of his mouth gave him away.

"Cute?" she asked.

"Not cute, exactly, but —" at that moment,

the manager called her to get to work. Reluctantly, she got up.

"Tell me about it later, please. I love you, Daniel. Be careful on your way home." She kissed Daniel good-bye, but his thoughts were still on her earlier question.

Not exactly cute, really, he thought. No, Ali was more like *beyond* cute. With that resolved, he finished his dumplings and left to ride home.

On an isolated stretch of road, Daniel heard the sound he had been dreading — the sound of dirt bikes.

Solemnly, and with the same precision Daniel had seen at the dojo that afternoon, Johnny and the Cobras surrounded Daniel with their dirt bikes. Inch by inch as they rode down the road, they forced his bicycle toward the edge of the pavement.

"I'm sorry about the pie, okay?" said Daniel, pleading.

Johnny's answer was to force Daniel closer to the edge.

"I don't want to fight." Johnny just stared at him. "Please."

Silently, Johnny brushed Daniel's bicycle to the limit and then he pulled away. Daniel tumbled down the embankment and his bike followed him, clattering through the brush.

The last Daniel saw of Johnny that night was the tail light of his dirt bike, receding in the darkness.

Chapter
Eight

"KIAAIIIII!" Daniel howled in disgust as he heaved his broken bicycle into the dumpster outside his apartment.

He had walked it all the way home, but when the axle broke in the parking lot, he gave up on it.

Daniel's mother was just getting out of the Chevy when she saw Daniel at the dumpster.

"Daniel!" she called, running across the lot to him. "What's the matter?" He turned away from her to hide the tears and the bruises.

"What's wrong with your bike? Why did you throw it away?"

"Felt like it," he mumbled.

His mother was firm.

"Face me when I'm talking to you, please."

Reluctantly, Daniel turned to his mother. She gasped when she saw the new scratches and his torn clothing.

"All right. I've had it," she said. "I want to know what's going on."

"Well, what do you want to hear?" he challenged her.

"The truth."

"You don't want to hear the truth."

"Yes, I do," she insisted.

"No, all you want to hear is how great it is in this Garden of Eden!" Daniel was angry, angry at his mother, angry at Ali, angry at Johnny, and even angry at himself. He had hit his boiling point. He continued.

"It might be great for *you*, but it *stinks* for me. I hate it here. I *hate* it! Do you understand? I just want to go back home, okay? Not to some phony Garden of Eden — just plain *home*! Newark!"

As he finished talking, the tears began — real ones. He turned away from Lucille. Gently, Lucille reached for him, turning him towards her. She used her handkerchief to clean the scratches on his forehead.

"I can't help if you won't tell me," she invited.

"I've got to take karate."

"You *took* karate."

"I mean at a dojo — a real school. Not the YMCA."

"Daniel, fighting won't solve anything."

"Neither will palm trees," he retorted.

"That's not fair."

Daniel's anger at his mother erupted.

"Like moving here was fair without even

asking me how I felt about it? Right? That was fair?"

"You're right — I should have asked. I'm sorry."

" 'I'm sorry' doesn't help, Ma. I want to go *home*. I don't understand the rules here."

"You know, hon. I'm not so sure I understand them myself. It's been a little rocky here for me, too, though *I've* made it through three days without getting a black eye." Daniel caught the twinkle in her eye and smiled in spite of himself.

"Come on," she continued. "Let's get you cleaned up and we'll see if we can't figure out the rules together." She put her arm around Daniel's shoulder and they began to walk to the apartment together.

"Say, what about your bike?" she asked.

"It's a goner. Besides," he answered, "I'll be safer on a bus."

Chapter
Nine

It couldn't be, but it *was*. Daniel found his bicycle, good as new, standing outside the front door when he got home from school one afternoon.

He knew his mother couldn't have fixed it — she couldn't hang a picture, much less repair a bike — nor could she have afforded to have it repaired. Curious, Daniel went to Mr. Miyagi's workroom.

Daniel found the old man seated at his work table, surrounded by bonsai trees, trimming one with the utmost concentration. He glanced at Daniel through the branches of the wizened miniature.

Daniel approached him softly. There was a contagious sense of serenity about this old man and his room.

"Did you fix my bike?"

Mr. Miyagi smiled and nodded.

"Thank you."

"Welcome," Mr. Miyagi said and then returned his attention to trimming branches. Daniel watched, frankly curious.

"Are these real?" he asked.

"Hai."

"How'd they get so small?"

Mr. Miyagi answered proudly. "I train, clip here, tie there. Bonsai grows."

"Where'd you learn how? Japan?"

"Okinawa. That's my country. It is a small island, southwest of main islands of Japan, halfway to China."

"Did you learn this kind of gardening in a school there?" Daniel asked, as he touched the soft needles of the miniature pine.

"No, my father. He taught me."

"He was a gardener?"

"Fisherman."

It seemed odd to Daniel that a fisherman could learn such an incredible skill and pass it on to his son. Yet, there it was.

"They're really beautiful," he remarked.

"You like to try it?"

"Thanks, but I'd just mess it up."

"Close eyes," said Mr. Miyagi, quietly.

Daniel hesitated, but there was something reassuring in Mr. Miyagi's face. He shut his eyes.

"Now concentrate. Think only of a tree. Make it a perfect picture — every detail down to last leaf. Wipe mind clean of everything but tree. Nothing exists in whole world but tree. Just tree."

He saw it. It stood, a cypress, on a cliff by

an ocean, beaten and shaped by the harsh wind and salt air. Its branches withstood the environment and reached bravely for nourishment and survival. It was lonely and beautiful.

"You got it?"

Daniel nodded.

"Open eyes. Remember picture?"

"Yes."

Mr. Miyagi pushed a small bushy pine tree to him and placed the clippers in Daniel's hand.

"Make like picture," he said, returning to his own tree.

Daniel stared at the tree in front of him, overwhelmed by the task. Mr. Miyagi sensed his awe, and smiled.

"Trust the picture."

"But how do I know if my picture is the right one?"

"If it comes from inside you, it's always the right one."

It seemed so simple. Could it be true? Tentatively, Daniel snipped at the tree. And again. He looked at Mr. Miyagi for approval. When he nodded, Daniel turned his full attention to the tree.

An hour later, Daniel's mother came into the maintenance room, amused to find her son pruning tiny trees.

"Hi," she said, entering the room.

"Hey, Mom, look!"

"You fixed your bike?"

"No, Mr. Miyagi fixed it."

"Oh," she said turning to him. "Thank you very much. How much do we owe you?"

"My pleasure."

"Well, thank you."

"Welcome." Mr. Miyagi bowed to her. She smiled and bowed awkwardly in return. Then she came over to where Daniel was working.

"What are you doing?"

"Trimming. How do you like these baby trees?"

"Bonsai tree," Mr. Miyagi corrected Daniel.

"They are beautiful," she said, admiring them.

"Mr. Miyagi learned how to do this in Okinawa. That's where he comes from."

"Really, they're something."

Mr. Miyagi smiled at her and presented her with a bonsai.

"For me? Oh, no — I couldn't." But Mr. Miyagi insisted.

"Please. Hurt feelings if you don't accept."

She was touched by his obvious sincerity and took the tree, thanking him again. Then, she turned to Daniel.

"Come on, we've got to go. It's getting late and tomorrow's a school day."

"I'll be up in half an hour."

"No, it's time to go now," she insisted. "Mr. Miyagi, thank you for everything — really." He smiled warmly. As Daniel stood up to leave with his mother, Mr. Miyagi picked up Daniel's tree and put it in his arms.

"No forget tree. Practice."

He slipped the clippers into Daniel's pocket.

"Thanks."

"Welcome. Sayonara," he bowed. Daniel and his mother bowed in return.

Daniel was pleased and excited by the events of the evening. He admired his mother's bonsai.

"Boy, Mom. He gave you the best one. Aren't they something? Look, the bike works perfectly, too."

Daniel thought again of the first time he'd seen Mr. Miyagi, trying to catch a fly with chopsticks. Somehow, now, that didn't seem quite as strange as it had at first. It was certainly no stranger than knowing, beyond doubt, that if it comes from inside you, it's always right.

Chapter
Ten

BEING a live worm is better than being a dead duck.

That was something Daniel told himself often over the next six weeks while he practiced karate with his book. He could practice a kick now without having to hold the wall, but still he wasn't nearly good enough to face Johnny. So, he learned Johnny's class schedule and avoided him. That made Daniel feel like a worm. A live one.

On Halloween, Daniel sat on the stairs of the apartment and watched Freddy and his friends, garbed in bizarre costumes, depart for the dance at the high school. That made Daniel think of Ali. Would she be there? He'd never know.

Those were lonely thoughts and Daniel needed company. He thought of his bonsai tree and how he had pruned it and clipped it so that it almost looked like the picture in his mind — the one thing that flourished in this Garden of Eden. On an impulse, Daniel went to look for Mr. Miyagi.

He found him in his workroom, carving a small pumpkin with a charming Oriental face.

"Ah, Danielsan. Hello. Long time, no see."

"Yeah, well, I've been busy."

"Happy Halloween," he said, tossing Daniel a small bag of candy. "How bonsai coming?"

"Pretty good."

"I pass by high school. Big doings going on. Not going?"

"No," Daniel answered.

"How come?"

"Don't feel like it."

"Danielsan, you too much by yourself. It's no good."

"I'm not by myself. I'm with you."

Mr. Miyagi nodded in understanding, but then said, "To make honey, young bee need young flower. Not old prune."

Daniel laughed. "I don't have a costume, anyway."

"If you had costume, would you go?"

"Uh, remember those bike accidents?"

"Hai."

"They weren't accidents. So, unless I go as the Invisible Man, I'm better off staying here."

"No can make invisible, but can shroud

you in curtain of mystery. Sometimes handy-man very handy, Danielsan." Mr. Miyagi was up and rummaging in his back room.

Less than an hour later, a shower entered the high school gym where the dance was in progress. Mr. Miyagi had fashioned a costume for Daniel out of aluminum piping, a shower head and flowered curtain so that Daniel was completely covered.

Through a crack in the curtain, he looked around the crowded gym until he saw Ali dressed as a harem girl. The costume showed off some of her best features. Carefully, Daniel maneuvered the shower to her side, quickly opened the curtain, enveloped her and closed the curtain. Ali was startled, but smiled when she recognized her captor.

"Want to dance?" he asked, putting his arms around her waist.

"I never danced with a shower before," she said, putting her arms around his neck.

"Well, don't you think it's time to test the water?" he joked.

Ali nodded, smiling. "Where have you been hiding? I haven't seen you for weeks."

"I've been busy."

"I'm glad you got *un*busy," Ali said.

"Me, too."

Daniel looked into Ali's eyes, then pulled her softly toward his racing heart. She looked up at him and tilted her head. Gently, he leaned toward her and they kissed. And kissed again.

Together, they realized it was getting very steamy in the shower.

"Want to go outside?" Ali asked. Daniel nodded and they began the awkward journey, moving a crowded shower outside, laughing and peeking through the curtain to navigate.

Before they got to the door, however, some joker lobbed a raw egg over Daniel's shower curtain. It landed on Daniel's head and dribbled down his face and ears. Ali laughed and so did Daniel, in spite of himself.

"What a time to need a shower," he said. "Look, I've got to get cleaned up. I'll be back in a few minutes. Don't go making a splash with anyone else while I'm gone, okay?"

"No sweat. You're the only shower in *my* life. You're the mainstream to me. Compared to you, all the other guys are just drips!" Ali assured him.

Daniel felt happy all the way from his head to his toes as he walked to the boys' locker room. He was glowing.

How could anything ever go wrong now that he had a neat girl like Ali on his side?

Chapter
Eleven

IT seemed like such a good idea at the time that Daniel just couldn't resist it. If only it had turned out the way he'd hoped.

It began as he was cleaning the egg off himself in the shower room, still protected by the anonymity of his own shower curtain when he heard Johnny and Bobby talking.

"You ready?" Bobby asked.

"In a minute," answered Johnny.

"I'll get the guys," said Bobby, walking out, leaving Daniel alone in the bathroom with Johnny who was in a stall. Telltale puffs of smoke emerged at the top of the stall. Daniel checked and saw they were alone. He would have walked out himself, glad to escape conflict with Johnny if he hadn't had the bright idea.

He spotted a hose at the utility sink nearest the stall where Johnny sat smoking. Within seconds, he had the hose strung over the light fixtures and pointed directly above Johnny's head. Daniel hesitated for a moment before turning on the water. He considered the possibility that this was a dumb idea, but then he rejected it, confident he could escape unidentified. Revenge was his.

He turned the cold water on hard, stood still long enough to hear Johnny's shout, and then ran like crazy — right into the arms of the Cobras who were returning to the bathroom for a smoke.

Daniel didn't waste a second. He broke loose from Bobby's grasp and headed for the gym. He could hear Johnny yelling after him.

"Stop that creep!"

With all the Cobras chasing after him, including a soaking wet Johnny, Daniel tore through the crowd in the gym, past an astonished Ali. He glanced over his shoulder just before going through the door. The last thing he saw was Ali, sticking out her beautiful leg to trip Johnny.

What a girl! Daniel thought, shedding his shower costume as he went. He knew his only hope for safety was to get over the chainlink fence at the far end of the athletic field. If he could do that, he'd be able to get home. If he couldn't, well, he didn't want to think about it.

He ran across the empty field. The fence was closer now, but he was winded and tired. At last, he reached the fence and scrambled up it, struggling to reach the top, but before he could pull himself over, Johnny grabbed him from behind and pulled him to the ground.

He landed on the turf with a thud and found himself surrounded by Cobras. Daniel made one last, desperate attempt to break away, dodging under Johnny's grasp and kicking at his tormenters, but Johnny's knee landed square in his chest and ended all hope of escape. Daniel crumpled to the ground, sitting with his back to the fence.

Johnny stood in front of him, soaking wet. He put his hands on his hips and spoke, icy with anger, "You couldn't leave well enough alone, could you, you little twerp, and now you're going to pay for it!"

Daniel had the sickening feeling that aviator's glasses weren't going to hide the damage this time.

The Cobras uncoiled and struck at him, pushing him against the fence. Johnny led the pack with his vicious kicks, and soon, Daniel was flat on the ground.

"Get him up," said Johnny gruffly.

"Come on, man," Bobby said. "He's had it. Leave him alone."

In his haze, Daniel realized that Johnny had not heard Bobby. Robotlike, Johnny stood in front of Daniel and spoke, "A man faces you, he is your enemy. An enemy deserves no mercy. Get him up."

Daniel recognized the tone of the recitation at the Cobra Kai Dojo. He was too beat to be terrified. He only hoped it wouldn't last long.

Two of the Cobras pulled Daniel to his feet and propped him against the fence. Johnny backed away from him to leave room for a running leap.

Through blurred vision, Daniel watched Johnny's lethal side kick unfolding at him. Too weak to move, he waited for the inevitable impact.

But it never came.

From out of nowhere, a figure leaped over the fence and pushed Daniel out of the way. A split second later, Johnny's foot dented the fence where Daniel had been.

Daniel watched, vaguely aware, as a small lithe figure obscured by shadows, crouched opposite the Cobras in a low cat stance. The Cobras attacked the anonymous defender, but were quickly repelled by a series of precision punches and kicks. Finally, the mystery figure somersaulted toward Johnny, coming out of the crouch to attack face to face with a single kick so powerful that Johnny was downed instantly, groaning in pain.

That was the last thing Daniel saw before he lost consciousness.

Chapter
Twelve

DANIEL became aware of two things simultaneously: the bright lights of Mr. Miyagi's workroom and the repugnant smell of a compress on his head. He closed his eyes against the lights and removed the foul-smelling towel.

"Leave on," said Mr. Miyagi, replacing it firmly.

"It stinks," Daniel protested.

"Smell bad. Heal good," said Mr. Miyagi, turning his attention to Daniel's other wounds, dabbing gently and bandaging as necessary.

Slowly, Daniel recalled the scene by the fence. He didn't know how he'd gotten to Mr. Miyagi's workroom, but he *did* know how he'd survived. Eager to thank his rescuer, he looked around the room.

"Where's the other guy?"

Mr. Miyagi continued his work.

"You know, Mr. Miyagi, the one who —"

Mr. Miyagi blinked. Then Daniel knew, as sure as anything that ever came from within him, that there wasn't another guy — that Mr. Miyagi was the mystery figure who had saved him by the fence.

"You?" Daniel said in awe.

Mr. Miyagi smiled and bowed. He then poured two cups of tea. Daniel pulled himself up slowly, relieved that he could sit up at all.

"Why didn't you tell me?"

"What?"

"That you knew karate?"

"Never asked," Mr. Miyagi answered simply.

"Where'd you learn?"

"From father."

"The fisherman?"

"All Miyagi know two things," he explained. "Fish and karate. Karate come from Okinawa. As a matter of fact, Danielsan, Miyagi ancestors bring from China in sixteenth century. Then it was called 'Te.' 'Te' mean 'hand.' Later, fancy-pants uncle call it Kara-te. Empty hand. No weapon, see?"

"I thought it came from Buddhist temples and stuff."

"You watch too much TV." He removed the compress, rinsed it, and replaced it on Daniel's head.

"Have *you* ever taught anyone karate?" Daniel asked.

"No. No have son."

"Would you teach someone?"

"Depend."

"On what?"

"Reason."

"How do you like revenge for a reason?" Daniel challenged.

"Danielsan," Mr. Miyagi spoke firmly. "If man look for revenge with karate, best he start by digging *two* graves."

"At least I would have company," Daniel said wryly.

"Fighting always last answer to problem."

Daniel wished it were as simple as this old man seemed to think. Fighting was the one thing he didn't want to do, but he didn't seem to have any choice in the matter.

"No offense, Mr. Miyagi, but I don't think you understand the problem."

"Oh, yes. Understand perfect. Friends karate students, right?"

"Yeah."

"Problem is attitude."

"No, Mr. Miyagi. The problem is that I get my butt kicked every time I look at those guys."

"Yes. Because boys learn wrong attitude. Karate used for defense."

"That's not what they're taught."

"I can see that. No such thing as bad student. Only bad teacher. Teacher say. Student do."

"Right, Mr. Miyagi," said Daniel sarcastically. "That's the solution, then. I'll just toodle over to their school and straighten out the sensei!"

"*Now* you use head for something beside target, Danielsan! Good! More tea?"

Daniel nodded. "I was only kidding. Getting my butt kicked by Johnny is one thing, but getting it kicked by his teacher, Kreese, is another. He'd kill me."

"Get killed anyway."

Mr. Miyagi had a way of getting right to the point.

"Would you come with me?"

Mr. Miyagi shook his head vigorously.

"No can do."

"Hey *you* said it was a good idea."

"For you, yes. For me, number one rule is no like to get involved."

"But you're *already* involved," said Daniel, and he could see that Mr. Miyagi knew he was right.

"So sorry," he said, returning to his tea.

"Well, thanks for nothing. I didn't have enough trouble before. Now I've got to carry your weight, too. If you had let those guys beat me, it would be over. Now, they're going to want revenge and all you can say is 'so sorry.' Well, so am I!" Daniel stalked out of the workroom.

Halfway down the walkway, Daniel heard Mr. Miyagi call him. He turned.

"Okay, I go, too."

A feeling of relief swept over Daniel. He smiled and thanked Mr. Miyagi. Then another thought occurred to him.

"Say, Mr. Miyagi, what belt do you have?"

Mr. Miyagi looked at his waist and tugged at his belt.

"Canvas," he said. "You like?"

Daniel was surprised that Mr. Miyagi could have misunderstood the question.

"Sure, it's a nice belt, but —"

"J.C. Penney, $3.98," he said proudly.

"No, Mr. Miyagi — I mean it's great, but —"

"Danielsan, in Okinawa, belt mean 'don't need rope to hold up pants.' Karate here — in head —" he pointed. "Not here — in belt. Understand?"

Daniel nodded.

"Good night, Danielsan."

"Good night, Mr. Miyagi."

Slowly, Daniel made his way back to his apartment, thinking about Mr. Miyagi — this man who seemed to be able to turn his world upside down with a few words. He had much to learn, he knew. He wondered if he could learn it from Mr. Miyagi.

Chapter
Thirteen

KREESE paced through the ranks of his students at the dojo.

"Lose concentration in a fight and you're dead meat, understand?"

"Yes, sensei," shouted the students in unison. Daniel and Mr. Miyagi sat silently in the gallery watching the class. Kreese continued.

"We do not train to be merciful. Mercy is for the weak. Here, or on the street, or in competition, if a man confronts you, he is your enemy. An enemy deserves no mercy."

A chill ran down Daniel's spine, as he recalled the last time he'd heard those words.

The students paired for combat practice and, for the first time since he'd arrived in California, Daniel had an opportunity to observe a karate match without being an unwilling participant. There was an awesome beauty in the grace and speed of the motions, but even with hand and foot protectors, it was a rough game. One of the students was downed by another and was in obvious pain.

Kreese was not sympathetic.

"Get up," he said, coldly. "Pain purifies. The mind is master."

The boy gasped for breath, trying to pull himself up. To Daniel, he didn't appear purified — merely petrified.

"Say it!" commanded Kreese.

Weakly, the boy repeated Kreese's phrase.

"Louder!"

"Pain purifies. The mind is master!" he shouted. Kreese nodded and ordered the injured boy to do a hundred sit-ups. The boy dragged himself to the sit-up board and began the task.

It was at this point that Johnny spotted Daniel and Mr. Miyagi in the gallery. Kreese observed Johnny's distraction and said, sarcastically, "Lose concentration and you're dead meat, Mr. Lawrence."

Johnny leaned forward and whispered to Kreese. The sensei's hard eyes focussed on Daniel and Mr. Miyagi. Daniel was unnerved by his look and began to stand up.

"Let's go," he whispered to Mr. Miyagi, but the old man's hand rested gently on his knee, staying him. Kreese walked to the edge of the gallery and stood before Mr. Miyagi, towering over him.

"I understand you jumped on my student last night."

"Think you got facts mixed up," Mr. Miyagi replied, evenly.

"You calling my boy a liar?"

"Not calling anyone name." said.

"What are you here for, old man?"

"Ask to leave boy alone."

"What's the matter?" Kreese sneered. "He can't take care of his own problems?"

"One to one problem, yes. Four to one problem, too much to ask anyone."

Kreese laughed.

"That's what's bothering you? The odds? We can fix that. Feel like a match, Mr. Lawrence?"

"Anytime, sensei." Johnny snapped to attention.

Daniel felt the burn of Kreese's stare as he eyed him. Somehow, he managed to keep his face still and hide the terror he felt in the presence of this man and his deadly students.

"Roberts!" commanded Kreese. "Get him a gi! We'll have a match. That better, old man?"

"No."

"Well," he said, sarcastically. "What more can we do to accommodate you? Room service?"

"No more fighting."

"This is a karate dojo, not a knitting class," he said as he thrust the karate outfit into Daniel's arms. "Now, let's get this over with. I've got a class to teach!"

Mr. Miyagi took the gi from Daniel's hand

and put it neatly on the chair. He turned to leave. Daniel followed.

Kreese's face reddened in anger. He blocked their exit and spoke menacingly.

"You don't come into my dojo, drop a challenge, and leave, old man. Now, get the kid on the floor, or, antique or not, you and I have a serious problem."

"Too much advantage, your dojo."

"Name a place," Kreese challenged.

Mr. Miyagi's eyes flicked to the bulletin board by the door. For the first time, Daniel noticed the poster: ALL VALLEY UNDER 18 OPEN KARATE CHAMPIONSHIP. He got a sinking feeling when Mr. Miyagi pointed to it. He'd been humiliated by Johnny in public once — at the beach. Once was enough. He wanted to protest, but somehow the words wouldn't come. While he was trying to speak, Kreese's face lit up and he began to laugh.

"You got real guts, old man. Real guts!" The students were laughing as well. Kreese turned to Johnny.

"Mr. Lawrence, we'll go for that, right?"

"Yes, sensei," said Johnny, humorlessly.

With exaggerated politeness, Kreese addressed Mr. Miyagi again.

"Are there any other accommodations I can make for you, sir — you or this 'student'?"

"Want student left alone, to train."

"Pushy little fella, aren't you? Okay. No one from here lays a hand on the prima donna until the tournament. Got that, men?"

"Yes, sensei," they answered in unison.

"But, hear this, old man. If you and the kid don't show at the tournament, it's open season on him. And you."

Mr. Miyagi bowed politely and went to the door. Daniel followed close on his heels. When the door closed, Daniel found his voice.

"Mr. Miyagi, are you crazy? What did you go and do that for? I'm going to get beat up but good this time. You said we were going to find a solution!"

"Did," Mr. Miyagi said calmly as he proceeded to their truck. Daniel looked at him, astonished. He saw no solution on the horizon.

"Saved three months beating," Mr. Miyagi said, tossing him the keys.

Well, thought Daniel. *That* was true — maybe.

Chapter Fourteen

DANIEL was still quivering with fear and anger as he maneuvered the truck along the dirt road as Mr. Miyagi instructed. In spite of his anger at Mr. Miyagi, he recognized a certain logic in the situation. Too, he found himself proud to be allowed to drive Mr. Miyagi's truck, to be allowed in the old man's protection. Even with Mr. Miyagi's obvious peculiarities, Daniel really liked the man — really wanted to gain his respect. That came from inside him.

He pulled the truck up in front of an old ramshackle cabin in an abandoned oil rig area. Several old cars sat in the yard. Curious, Daniel got out of the truck with Mr. Miyagi and asked, "Where are we?"

"Miyagi's house." Astonished, Daniel laughed.

"I didn't know you were in the oil business!"

Mr. Miyagi ignored the sarcasm.

"Not everything is as it seems."

"What are we doing here?"

"Start training," Mr. Miyagi said, walking toward the cabin.

So it was as simple as that, thought Daniel. No more hours with a book in one hand and a wall in the other. He had his own sensei — and a rather odd dojo, it seemed.

He tried to look around, but it was hard to see his surroundings in the faded light of dusk. Suddenly, however, the yard was bathed in light by a series of spotlights that Mr. Miyagi had turned on. Daniel found himself surrounded by vintage automobiles. There was a 1948 DeSoto, a 1952 Studebaker, a Nash Rambler, 1956 — even an old "woody" station wagon. But the one that caught his eye was the 1950 Chevy convertible. Daniel opened the door and climbed in the driver's seat. Resting his elbow on the window and holding the steering wheel with his right hand, he wondered how the car must have felt to drive.

Daniel was so carried away by his fantasy that he didn't notice Mr. Miyagi until he came to the car. Embarrassed, Daniel climbed down and brought himself back to karate.

"You really think I can beat Johnny?"

"Doesn't matter," said Mr. Miyagi. "Attitude of his teacher is that only important thing is fist. That stupid, but is a fact of life. You show good fight, win, lose, no matter, you get respect. No more bother."

"Yeah — or they'll bury me where I fall."

"Either way, problem solved," Mr. Miyagi said, almost too matter-of-factly. Daniel found it an unnerving thought, but Mr. Miyagi continued, "Ready?"

"I guess so."

"Danielsan," said Mr. Miyagi sternly. "When you walk on road, if you walk on left side, it safe. If you walk on right side, safe, too. If you walk in middle, sooner or later you get squished like a grape. Same thing with karate. Either do karate 'yes,' or do karate 'no.' Do karate 'guess so,' you looking to get squished like a grape. Understand?"

"Yes," Daniel nodded, as the full meaning sank in. "I'm ready."

"Good. First step is sacred deal. I teach karate, that my part. You learn, that your part. I say. You do. No question. Deal?"

Deal, thought Daniel and reached to shake hands with his teacher. For the first time, though, he noticed that Mr. Miyagi was holding a bucket of soapy water, a sponge, and several towels in his hands. Before he knew what was happening, Mr. Miyagi unceremoniously slapped the soapy sponge into Daniel's extended hand. Then, he pointed to the cars in the yard and said, "Good. First wash. Then wax. Like this," making small clockwise circles with his right hand. "Wax on, right. Breathe in, breathe out."

Daniel watched, surprised, as he continued.

"Wax off, left," he said, making counterclockwise circles with his left hand. "Breathe in, breathe out — very important, breathe in breathe out." Mr. Miyagi turned and walked into the house before Daniel could ask any questions.

For someone who lets his cars get as dirty as these, thought Daniel, he sure is fussy about how they get cleaned. Daniel knew what karate lessons cost in a dojo and he had wondered how he would pay Mr. Miyagi. It looked like this was Mr. Miyagi's answer.

With that, Daniel turned to the Chevy, slapped the sponge onto the fender and began rubbing back and forth. From behind, Mr. Miyagi reached over to guide Daniel's hand in the prescribed circular motion.

"Breathe in — out. In — out."

Three-and-a-half hours later, Daniel wiped the last excess of wax from the last car. They all shined like new. Proudly, he put the cleaning gear away and went to get Mr. Miyagi for inspection. As he entered the house, though, he saw the old man sitting cross-legged in a meditative position, hands placed on knees, eyes closed, solemn.

Embarrassed, Daniel turned to leave lest he interrupt the ritual. Just as he turned the doorknob, however, he heard a sound. Surprised, he turned. As if on cue, Mr. Miyagi did it again. It was a snore. A very loud one.

Daniel left the old man sound asleep.

Chapter
Fifteen

SNORING, recalled Daniel, as he stood by his locker the next day.

He was brought from his recollections by Ali's presence. She was upset when she saw his bruises and turned to walk away.

"Hey. Where are you going?"

"To find King Jerk," she said. "This has got to stop."

"It's been taken care of," Daniel assured her.

"Oh, sure, I can see that."

"Listen, Ali," he said, stepping in front of her. "You can only make it worse for me." Ali stopped. "Come on," he invited. "Let's get you to class." He took Ali's hand and turned, spotting the Cobras standing behind them.

"Let's go," he said firmly, walking past Johnny and his friends.

As they passed, Tommy sneered and said,

"Must be 'Take Your Worm for a Walk Week.'" However, no one moved to stop Daniel and Ali. Ali looked at him, surprised.

"See? We got an agreement."

"So? What is it?"

"Easy. They promised not to beat up on me any more and I promised not to get blood on their clothes." Ali shook her head, laughing.

"You're unreal."

"So what am I supposed to do? Weep and moan?"

"Anybody else would."

"Who'd listen?"

Ali lifted her head to look straight into his eyes and smiled — that wonderful smile.

"Me," she said simply.

He felt so close to her. It was almost like at the dance — in the shower costume together. This time, though, instead of kissing her, he spoke.

"Well, uh, would you like to listen, say on Saturday night?"

"Sure" she said, jotting her address on a piece of paper for him. "Bye." Quickly, she brushed his lips with hers and turned to go into her classroom.

Daniel floated down the hall towards his next class. As he turned the corner, he was brought down to earth by bumping into Johnny. Johnny looked at the paper Ali had given Daniel, still in his hand.

"Don't push it, punk," said Johnny, trying to grab the paper. Daniel carefully evaded

Johnny's grasp, but realized it was going to be a losing battle. Johnny *was* bigger. Out of the corner of his eye, Daniel spotted one of his teachers.

"Mr. Harris," he called. "Can I talk to you a minute?" Johnny's hands obediently went to his side, as Mr. Harris turned to the duo, looking a little puzzled.

"LaRusso," Daniel supplied. "I'm in your third period history class. I really got a lot out of that lecture you gave about how Indians got their horses."

Mr. Harris smiled.

"That's nice to hear," he said.

"Yeah, well, I was trying to explain to my friend here how the stuff all fit together with colonization and all that. But, then I messed up. So, could you give us a quick review?"

Mr. Harris was clearly flattered.

"I'm free this period. How about you?" he asked.

Daniel looked invitingly at Johnny who said, "I've got a class. But thanks anyway." With that, he turned and stalked off.

Daniel smiled, relieved.

Chapter
Sixteen

DANIEL was startled by the perfection of the garden. A small path drew his eyes along the bed of a small stream past beautiful rocks and plants. Three trees seemed somehow perfectly placed around a gentle waterfall. Traditional Japanese lanterns stood on cedar poles at the perimeter. A few benches invited a visitor to rest and contemplate. What a strange place to find behind Mr. Miyagi's ramshackle house, thought Daniel.

But there it was, and at the back of the house Mr. Miyagi was just putting the last few nails into a new wooden deck.

"Hey, this is beautiful!" said Daniel.

Ignoring the compliment, Mr. Miyagi invited Daniel to kneel on the deck. Daniel knelt and picked up a strange wooden block with a leather strap on it.

"What's this?"

"Japanese sander."

"How does it work?"

Solemnly, Mr. Miyagi answered, "Funny you should ask," attaching the sander to Daniel's hand with the leather strap. He showed him how to make perfect circles with the sandpaper on the rough wood deck.

"Wouldn't it be easier to go back and forth?"

"Hai. But you go circle." He rose and walked into the house, leaving Daniel with a stack of fresh sandpaper and a large, unsanded deck. Daniel was disappointed. He wished he knew what the purpose was in these chores. But he'd made the promise to Mr. Miyagi and he couldn't question his teacher.

Daniel was near the end of his task when Mr. Miyagi appeared on the finished portion of the deck with a hibachi. Soon there was a charcoal fire burning in it and the wonderful smell of cooked fish spurred Daniel to finish quickly. He was very hungry when he saw Mr. Miyagi take the finished meal inside. Hurriedly, Daniel completed the sanding and tidied up, mopping his sweaty face and chest with his shirt. He rinsed off at a faucet by the side of the house and headed inside, hungry and expectant.

Mr. Miyagi greeted him at the door with a contented belch.

"Splinters gone?"

"Yeah," said Daniel, looking over the old man's shoulder to see one very empty plate at the table. He could barely hide his disappointment, but Mr. Miyagi apparently didn't notice it. He was too busy sliding back and forth on the deck, feeling for splinters with his feet.

"Good," he said. "Come morning. Six A.M." He bowed to Daniel and turned to go into the darkness of his garden. Daniel found himself bowing to the air. Perplexed, and somewhat hurt, he left for home.

After a good night's sleep, however, Daniel was feeling better. It seemed pointless to develop any resentment against Mr. Miyagi. Either he would teach Daniel karate or he would not. Nobody else was going to do it. In the meantime, Daniel decided, he sure was learning some funny ways to do things. Nobody sands in circles.

Engrossed in these thoughts, he entered Mr. Miyagi's house at six o'clock to find him exactly as he had found him the first time they met.

Snap! The chopsticks chased a wayward fly, missing. Daniel sat down to watch. After a moment, he asked, "Wouldn't a fly swatter be easier?"

"Ah, but man who can catch fly with chopstick can accomplish anything."

Why was it everything Mr. Miyagi said *seemed* so simple, thought Daniel. How could catching a fly with chopsticks mean so much? Daniel realized that the purpose wasn't to be victor over the fly, but to be victor over one's own weakness. Simple. Sort of.

"Ever catch one?" Daniel asked.

"Not yet."

"Can I try?"

Mr. Miyagi nodded to indicate another pair of chopsticks. Daniel took them and sat down cross-legged on the floor. He tried holding the chopsticks, but it was awkward at first. He'd always had trouble doing this to eat fried rice, and he wondered why he thought he could catch a fly with chopsticks. After a few minutes, though, he found that he could manipulate them — a bit. Then he began looking for a fly. Mr. Miyagi glanced at him from the corner of his eye, then turned his attention back to his own chopsticks.

Snap! Nothing.

Daniel watched as a fly approached him. Three feet, five feet, four feet, too high. Now closer, now closer, three feet, two-and-a-half, two —

Snap!

There, caught between Daniel's chopsticks, was a squirming fly.

Mr. Miyagi laid his own chopsticks down and stood up.

"Hey! Look at that, Mr. Miyagi, huh? Not bad for a kid from Newark!"

Miffed, Mr. Miyagi grunted, "Beginner's luck," and walked to the door. Daniel grabbed an imaginary telephone with his free hand.

"Hello?" he said. "Yes, sir. Ah, yes, sir. He's right here, sir. All right, sir." He cradled the phone and addressed the struggling fly.

"Okay, you're in luck. That was the governor. You got a reprieve — just in time, I might add." He stood and, still holding the fly, walked to the door. "Now, go on," he said to the fly. "No more in the house." He released his captive and walked over to Mr. Miyagi.

"Hey, Mr. Miyagi. Does that mean I can accomplish anything?"

Mr. Miyagi thought for a second, weighing his answer.

"Yes, but first paint fence," he said, handing Daniel a brush and indicating the open paint cans and the fence surrounding the garden. "Up — down. Up — down. All in wrist, see? Up — down. Breathe in, out. Don't forget."

He watched Daniel for a few moments to be sure he was going up — down and then walked into the house.

Three hours later, Daniel reentered the cabin. Mr. Miyagi was tending his ancient bonsai with the utmost concentration. Daniel interrupted him by flopping down on the mat near him.

"Finished," he said, relaxing as much as he could without smearing his paint-splattered clothes on the floor. Mr. Miyagi's attention, however, did not waver from his tree.

"Both sides?" he asked.

Frustrated, Daniel left to paint the other side. After all, he thought, he could do *any*-thing.

Chapter Seventeen

DANIEL began to get the full meaning of coming from "the Hills" as he walked up to Ali's door. To his right, in her driveway, was a Mercedes. To his left, in her neighbor's driveway, were *twin* Rolls Royces! Ali's house looked like something out of a movie set: big, gorgeous, opulent, and above all, intimidating. Daniel's mother sat at the wheel of the Chevy while Daniel went to the house.

Somehow, he made it to the doorbell and was relieved when Ali appeared. He wouldn't, after all, have known *what* to say if a butler had answered the door. But with Ali, it was easy.

"Hi."

"Hi." She smiled, joining him. Together, they walked toward the Chevy where his mother was waiting. Daniel hoped he could make it to the car and out of the neighborhood without further ado. No such luck.

A midnight-blue Mercedes pulled into the driveway. Two perfect people stepped out of the perfect car, wearing perfect tennis "whites." Daniel knew immediately these had to be Ali's parents. She introduced them.

"Mom, Dad, I'd like you to meet Daniel LaRusso."

They smiled and shook his hand, glancing dubiously at the very imperfect Chevy at the curb. Fleetingly, Daniel wondered if they might believe he was an antique car buff. Somehow, though, he didn't think the Chevy would convince them of that!

"Pleased to meet you," said Daniel uncomfortably.

"You live in Encino, Dan?" asked Mr. Mills.

Daniel shook his head.

"Well, where do you live?"

Daniel hesitated before he answered. He knew that no matter how he said it, Reseda would end up sounding like a hotbed of crime-ridden poverty. Well, next to *this*, anything was second rate.

"Reseda, sir," he said.

Ali's parents exchanged knowing looks.

"Don't be too late, dear," Mrs. Mills said, and they turned to walk into the house.

Daniel walked Ali to the Chevy.

"Mom, this is Ali Mills. Ali, this is my mother, Lucille LaRusso."

"I'm glad to meet you, Mrs. LaRusso," said Ali, offering her hand.

Daniel's mother took it. "Call me Lucille,"

she said, "everyone does." Ali smiled at her.

"Okay, where to?" asked Daniel's mother.

They agreed on Golf 'n' Stuff and Daniel's mother turned the key in the ignition. Nothing happened. She tried again. Nothing.

"Say, Ali," she said. "Can you drive?"

"Sure," Ali replied, matter-of-factly.

"Great," she said, moving out of the car to let Ali take the wheel. Daniel got out with her. "We'll push. You let it roll," she told Ali. "And when I say now, pop it. Okay?"

"Okay."

Daniel knew the drill. This had happened in Michigan. It had happened in Nevada. It had even happened in California, but it had *never* happened in front of Ali's house. He glanced over at the house and with a sinking feeling realized that the curtains on the ground floor were pulled back. Ali's perfect mother and father were watching them start their less than perfect car. He knew it was silly but he wanted to become invisible. Right then and there.

"Guess we should have brought the Rolls, huh?" said his mother with a grin.

Daniel shot her a murderous look as they began to push. Within about twenty yards the engine caught. Ali moved over, and they jumped in. He was afraid of what Ali would think of them but it didn't seem to bother her at all. Ali and his mother were busily talking about Chinese food, which, it turned out, Ali really loved. The rest of the trip to Golf 'n' Stuff was uneventful. What a girl, Daniel thought as he and Ali walked through the parking lot where his mother had dropped them off.

Daniel had never seen anything like that amusement park. Golf 'n' Stuff was hardly descriptive of the range of activities. And there had been nothing like it in Newark.

The first thing that greeted them was the giant water slide, but that required bathing suits.

"I mean, it's one thing to take a *shower* fully clothed," Ali said, recalling the Halloween costume, "but to swim?!" They both laughed, and Daniel felt his tension melt away. He took Ali's hand and they headed for the ticket booth.

A wonderful two hours later, after Cokes and a stop at the video arcade, the trampoline, miniature golf course, bumper cars, and the photography booth, they walked, hand in hand, to the parking lot where Daniel's mother had said she would pick them up.

"Ali, you're a magician," Daniel said. "This is the best time I've had since I got to California."

"Then we should go for a repeat performance," she said, turning to him in the dim light.

"Definitely," he said, putting his arms around her waist. "Next time with bathing suits, on the gia —"

Daniel was interrupted by the blare of a horn.

"How ya doin', Ali?" said a boy from behind the wheel of a new Corvette. Ali was startled, too.

"Oh, hi, Eddie. Wow," she said, looking at the car. "This is neat!"

"Just got it. Want a ride?"

"Some other time. Uh, Eddie, this is Daniel. Daniel, Eddie." The boys shook hands as a convertible with Johnny at the wheel pulled up beside Eddie's Corvette. Johnny and the couple with him admired Eddie's Corvette and called to Ali.

Daniel's heart sank. How, he wondered, could he ever compete with Corvettes and convertibles, as well as manicured lawns, perfect tennis outfits, and crystal clear swimming pools? How could Reseda compete with Encino Hills?

"Hello, Ali," said Johnny sweetly.

"Hello."

"We're going for a ride," said one of the girls. "Want to come, Ali?"

"No thanks. I'll see you tomorrow," Ali said politely.

Just then, Lucille LaRusso's Chevy pulled in behind Johnny's car and honked. Johnny observed this and teased, "Your friend can come, too, if his mommy will let him."

The kids laughed, but Ali just glared at Johnny. He stared back at her and then peeled out of the parking lot. Ali and Daniel turned to the Chevy.

"You could have gone," Daniel offered.

"I didn't want to."

"I mean," he said, trying to sound calm, "it's no big deal."

"Look, if I'd really wanted to go, I would have," she said, climbing into the car. Daniel was sure she was disappointed to be in this ancient Chevy instead of Johnny's classy convertible, and was only being polite to him.

At Ali's house, Daniel walked her to the door.

"So anytime you want to go sliding," she said, "just say abracadabra —"

"Yeah, I'll call you," said Daniel, withdrawn, upset, let down by the scene in the parking lot.

He turned.

"Wait a sec," Ali called. He walked back to her. She reached her hands to his lips and, magically, a piece of paper appeared. She handed it to him.

"How are you going to call the magician if you don't have her phone number?" she asked, and then, in an instant, was gone.

Maybe, just maybe, thought Daniel, he *could* conquer the Hills. But it *was* going to take some magic.

Chapter
Eighteen

DANIEL grabbed the note from the door of Mr. Miyagi's house, crumpled it, and threw it. It rolled off the porch and lay in the dirt. Daniel watched it for a few seconds, thinking about his promise to Mr. Miyagi not to question his teacher. Somehow he had felt sure that today was the day he would really start learning karate, but instead he'd found the note.

After a moment, his anger subsided. Then, he jumped down, picked up the piece of paper, and smoothed it out flat.

"Paint house. No up and down. Side side. One half left hand, one half right hand," he reread.

Somewhat reluctantly, Daniel concluded that he might as well paint the house, but he wasn't going to enjoy the work and he *wasn't* going to do any more. Daniel decided that as soon as Mr. Miyagi got there, he was going to get himself out of the household maintenance business.

For now, he opened a can of paint and began the work. Side to side. No up and down.

Daniel was almost finished when Mr. Miyagi drove into the yard and emerged from his truck, carrying a string of freshly caught fish in one hand, a pole in the other. Sullenly, Daniel continued painting.

"You miss a spot," said Mr. Miyagi, critically.

The hurt boiled over. Daniel's brush stopped in mid-stroke and he turned in anger.

"Why didn't you tell me you were going fishing?"

"Not here when I went," he answered.

"Maybe I would have liked to have gone, too. Ever think of that?"

"You doing karate training."

"Karate training?! I'm being your slave, *that's* what I'm doing. We made a deal."

"So?"

"So, you're supposed to teach and I'm supposed to learn. Remember? Or was there so much to be done on the house that you just forgot?" he said sarcastically, and then continued, "I haven't learned anything about karate."

"Learn plenty," Mr. Miyagi said calmly.

"Sure. How to sand your deck, paint your fence, wash your cars, paint your house.

What'll I learn next weekend? How to shingle the house? It could use it, you know."

"Not everything is as looks, Danielsan."

"Sure. This is really Buckingham Palace and you've got three thousand full-time handymen at work on it, right?"

With that, Daniel threw the paintbrush into the open can and stalked off to his bicycle.

"Danielsan," Mr. Miyagi called.

Daniel ignored him, lifting his bike to turn it around and leave without delay.

"Danielsan!"

Daniel was jolted by the command in Mr. Miyagi's voice. He stopped.

"Come here."

Daniel turned and walked over to Mr. Miyagi, facing him, towering over him, defying him.

"Show me how wax on, wax off."

Daniel stood still.

"Show!"

"I'm too tired. I can't lift my arms."

Mr. Miyagi rubbed his hands together in circles, faster and faster, until they seemed to be smoking. He walked behind Daniel and began to rub the muscles and sinews in his shoulders. Suddenly, Daniel felt sharp pressure on his tired muscles and, then, relief. It was amazing.

"Now show," said Mr. Miyagi. "On, off."

Slowly, Daniel lifted his arm and began to demonstrate the technique. Mr. Miyagi corrected the angle of his elbow.

"Show left, right. Left, right. Left, right."

Daniel felt the rhythm of the command and obediently mimicked the movements he knew so well, making perfect half-circles in the air.

Suddenly, Mr. Miyagi threw a chest punch at him. Before Daniel realized it, one of his circling hands intercepted the punch and deflected it, effortlessly. He looked at Mr. Miyagi, astonished and delighted. Mr. Miyagi's face revealed nothing.

"Sand floor," he ordered.

Obediently, Daniel showed the circles of the sanding motion. Mr. Miyagi made a slight correction to Daniel's gestures and then shot a kick to Daniel's stomach. Smoothly, Daniel deflected the kick with his sanding motion.

"Paint fence."

Up down. Up down. Up. Daniel's bent wrist caught Mr. Miyagi's head punch. On his downstroke, he parried a stomach punch.

Daniel could hardly contain his growing excitement as the full realization hit him. While he had been performing those perfectly ordinary chores for Mr. Miyagi, he'd also been gaining some extraordinary skills. Who would have thought — well, who *did* think? He'd been so busy building up resentment that he'd never stopped to think about what was going on. He was brought from his thoughts by Mr. Miyagi's voice.

"Wax on."

Mr. Miyagi fired a chest punch, which Daniel deflected easily, naturally.

"Wax off."

Again, the block was there.

"Paint up."

Daniel's snapping block was there to meet the attack.

"Down."

The heel of Daniel's palm caught the impact of Mr. Miyagi's fist.

"Side."

Daniel blocked again.

As Mr. Miyagi continued to fire commands, Daniel responded with errorless, effortless, blocking techniques, evading and deflecting all the punches and kicks Mr. Miyagi aimed at him with increasing speed.

"Side! — Sand! — On! — Off!"

Suddenly, at the height of the exercise, Mr. Miyagi stopped. Daniel, breathing hard and elated, waited for more.

Finally, Mr. Miyagi picked up his fish.

"Come tomorrow," he said, and disappeared into the house, slamming the door behind him.

Chapter
Nineteen

THE cold waters of the Pacific Ocean nipped at Daniel's toes as he thought about Ali. Ali at school, Ali on the soccer field, Ali on the beach, Ali with the cheerleaders, Ali on his mind. It was Monday after school and he would have to wait until Friday for their date. On Friday night at nine-thirty, he was meeting Ali at the country club after she'd had dinner with her parents. They'd go on the giant water slide. They'd play video games again. They'd — well, he told himself, don't think about that now.

"Okay. Go in now," Mr. Miyagi told him, bringing him out of his daydreaming.

Yes, Daniel remembered the cold waters again. Dutifully, he turned and walked in, knee deep. Almost immediately he was capsized by a wave. He emerged coughing and sputtering and looked to his teacher for sympathy.

"Not to worry. Will feel good."

"When?"

"When finish."

That was certainly true.

Time and again, the old man had shown that he knew what he was doing in Daniel's training. Daniel was confident that was true now. He just wished he could be out of the icy Pacific and into the familiar pool at the Y in Newark.

No, on second thought, he didn't wish that at all. He *didn't* want to go back to Newark. Between the friendship and respect he felt toward Mr. Miyagi, and his feeling — could it be love? — for Ali, he knew he really wanted to stay here in California. It wasn't going to be easy, but Daniel knew there was something special here for him.

He turned back to the Pacific and went in, bracing himself against the onslaught of the ocean. Following Mr. Miyagi's instructions he began throwing front kicks into the waves, fighting the undertow. Eventually, he found his rhythm and began his practice in earnest. The power and increasing persistence of the waves seemed perfectly suited for kick practice. It didn't feel good yet because it wasn't over, but it was satisfying to see such progress in his skills. When he was done, he sat on the beach, and wondered where Mr. Miyagi had gone.

At first, Daniel didn't see him because he was standing perfectly still on his left foot, perched like a sea gull on the top of a piling in the water — last remnant of an abandoned pier. A wave loomed toward Mr. Miyagi, so menacing that Daniel was ready to go to his rescue. But, at the instant it broke, Mr. Miyagi leaped high into the air, fired a kick with his left leg and landed, completely balanced on the piling in the same position in which he had started. It was awesome.

Later, Daniel's curiosity got the better of him; he had to ask Mr. Miyagi about it.

"What was that you were doing on the piling?"

"Crane technique."

"Does it work?"

"Do right, no can defense." Daniel could certainly believe that.

"Can you teach it to me?"

"First learn stand, then learn fly," Mr. Miyagi answered. Daniel was disappointed.

"Nature's rules, Danielsan, not mine."

Daniel knew he was right.

Chapter
Twenty

"NOT bad," said Daniel's mother admiringly.

Daniel had to agree, looking at himself in the mirror. Definitely casual but cool. White shirt over white pants — even white shoes. Definitely.

"Daniel, you know, I'm kind of tired tonight. I don't really want to chauffeur you and Ali." Daniel's heart fell. "So," she continued, "why don't you just take the car? Here are the keys." Overjoyed, Daniel kissed his mother on the cheek.

"Good-night, Mom. And thanks."

He left the house at 9:00.

By 9:15, he was waiting in the parking lot at the country club.

At 9:16, he realized, much to his dismay, that his casual but cool white-on-white look was identical to the uniform of the valet parking attendants at the club. Well, he thought, accepting a set of keys from a guest, this was probably going to be his only chance to drive a Mercedes. Dutifully, he parked the car in the lot and returned to the front of the club.

At 9:21, he parked a Rolls. Very carefully.

At 9:30, he stood patiently by the door.

At 9:40, he was still there.

At 9:45, he was anxious. Nervously, he walked to the rear of the club and discovered the open kitchen door. Because of his white camouflage, no one questioned his presence in the kitchen. Somehow, he found the door to the dining room and looked through it.

A wide circle of candlelit tables surrounded a small dance floor. On one side, an orchestra was pumping out a pathetic mimic of a disco beat. The dance floor was crowded with couples. Daniel tried to adjust his eyes to the dim light. Too soon, he succeeded. For there, on the dance floor, was Ali — dancing with Johnny.

Johnny's eyes met Daniel's. Ali's back was to the kitchen. Tenderly, Johnny put his hands on Ali's hair and tilted her face toward his. And then, as Daniel watched in horror, Johnny leaned down and kissed her.

Without thinking, Daniel spun around. He had to get out of there at any cost. As he turned, however, he rammed into an unsuspecting waiter, and both of them landed sprawled on the floor, while dishes clattered and crashed around them, mingling broken pottery with chicken kiev. Daniel scrambled to his feet, aware that all eyes in the dining room were on him. There was only one pair he cared about, though, and he locked eyes with Ali just before he ran out, through the kitchen, past the Mercedes, past the Rolls, past the Cadillacs and Lincolns, to the welcome and familiar 1969 Chevy station wagon.

Daniel didn't know until that moment that the old car could still leave rubber.

Chapter
Twenty-one

EVERY time Daniel let his concentration slip from the urgency of his bicycling, he thought again of the awful scene in the country club. Ali and Johnny. Johnny kissing Ali. If only he didn't care. But he did. With renewed conviction, he returned his attention to cycling.

He was only a little bit surprised to find that his furious cycling had brought him to Mr. Miyagi's house. He thought he had been riding aimlessly. What *did* surprise him was what he found there.

Weird, slurred singing drifted out into the night from inside the dark house. Daniel knocked on the front door, and the singing stopped. Slowly, the door opened. There stood Mr. Miyagi, reeking of Scotch, dressed in a World War II Army uniform, his chest covered with battle ribbons and medals.

"Am I disturbing you?" asked Daniel.

"Come in. Come in."

He ushered Daniel into the house, now strangely disheveled. A nearly empty bottle of Scotch stood on the low table, surrounded by yellowed newspaper clippings and framed photographs. Mr. Miyagi walked unsteadily to the table, poured two healthy shots of Scotch, and handed one to Daniel, clinking glasses.

"Kumpai," he said, downing the glass's contents. Daniel cautiously lifted his glass to his lips and winced at the sharp taste.

"Drink. Drink," insisted Mr. Miyagi. "Bad luck toast and then no drink. Banzai!"

"Like the little trees?" Daniel was confused.

"No. No. Not bonsai. *Banzai! Banzai!* Try."

"Banzai?"

"Banzai!"

"Banzai."

"Ah, good enough," said Mr. Miyagi, downing a second shot of Scotch. Obediently, Daniel swallowed his entire glass. The liquid burned, making him cough and sputter. Mr. Miyagi laughed, pounding Daniel's back good-naturedly, while refilling his own glass.

The scene had a surreal quality. Perhaps it was the strangeness of seeing the usually controlled old man so out of control. Daniel reached for reality.

"What are we celebrating?"

"Anniversary," Mr. Miyagi answered, proudly showing Daniel a yellowed picture of himself, much younger, but in the same uniform, with his arm around the shoulders of a lovely young Japanese girl.

"Wow! I didn't know you were married."

"Hai," nodded Mr. Miyagi. "Very beautiful. Don't you think?" Daniel nodded. "First time I see her in cane field. Hawaii. Beautiful. Very good cane cutter, too."

"Where is she now?" asked Daniel, a little afraid of the answer. Mr. Miyagi seemed unaware of Daniel's question as he walked to a cabinet and fetched another bottle of Scotch. Daniel looked for the answer on the table. He spotted a headline on a yellowed newspaper which brought him up, sharply.

JAPANESE AMERICANS INTERNED
PRESIDENT CITES WARTIME SECURITY

Daniel remembered studying that chapter of American history in school. For the duration of World War II, the Japanese Americans were taken from their homes and put into camps together. Frequently, their homes and property were seized or rendered valueless. The idea was that their sympathy might be more with America's enemies than with America. Also, they were told, some Americans might treat them badly. So, the camps were supposedly for their own protection.

To Daniel, that had always been a shameful part of America's history, but until that instant, it had been just that — history. With a jolt, Daniel realized that real people like Mr. Miyagi's wife had been interned while their men, like Mr. Miyagi, were battling for America. The irony of the situation cut like a knife. Yet, what had happened to Mrs. Miyagi?

Mr. Miyagi handed Daniel a picture of the young bride, this time alone and very pregnant, standing behind the barbed wire of an internment camp.

"Look at picture, Danielsan. To be first American-born Miyagi!"

Mr. Miyagi snapped to attention.

"Sergeant Miyagi reporting, sir." Clutching a tattered paper in his hand, he saluted an imaginary lieutenant, missing his mark and knocking his hat on the floor.

Daniel watched Mr. Miyagi's wobbly stance cause the medals on his chest to tremble. Daniel knew that those were the mark of a man who had fought as bravely in Europe as he had for Daniel.

Mr. Miyagi continued his monologue, which was now very garbled by Scotch.

"Sergeant Miyagi, regret to inform complication, *sir*. No doctor at camp, *sir*. Regret to inform mother child complication birth, *sir*. First American-born Miyagi. Home of free, land of brave." His voice trailed off, as his body sat heavily on his bed. He passed out.

"Mr. Miyagi?"

No answer.

Daniel stood and looked around, uncertain

what to do. He looked again at the newspapers on the table and found they were stories about the heroism and casualties of the Japanese-American troops on the European front.

Mr. Miyagi snored loudly and shifted his position, dropping his glass to the floor with a crash. Daniel walked over to him to be sure he'd be all right. He put his feet on the bed and pulled the blanket up on him tenderly — feeling suddenly as if they had changed places.

It was only as he took Mr. Miyagi's hat to put it on the table, that Daniel noticed his dog tags flopped across a particularly large medal. It was a Congressional Medal of Honor. It took Daniel's breath away.

Finally, Daniel pried Mr. Miyagi's fingers open and retrieved a telegram from them, reading:

"Department of War. We regret to inform you that on November 4, 1944, at the Manzinar Relocation Center, your wife and newborn son died due to complications arising from childbirth. Our sincerest condolences and sympathies."

Daniel looked down at the small crumpled figure snoring peacefully on the bed. He reached down and lovingly removed a thread from the old uniform, smoothing the silver hair. Daniel blew out the lantern, throwing the room into darkness, and left.

Chapter
Twenty-two

As soon as he rounded the corner, Daniel could see Ali standing by the school door, waiting for him, probably to make some kind of excuse about Friday night. Daniel didn't want to hear what Little Miss Country Club had to say.

He walked right past her into the school. He was tempted to turn when he heard her call, but he really didn't want to be hurt again. She ran up to him and stood in front of him.

"Daniel, I want to explain."

He winced when he saw a bandage on her hand, but it didn't stop him. He walked around her.

"Would you at least listen?"

"And be lied to?" He evaded her again.

"You're rude."

That stopped him. He turned on her in anger, "How can you tell? You live in a world of rude people. I just want *all* of you to leave me alone."

He stalked off, leaving Ali behind him. Somehow he felt that nothing he'd ever done hurt as much as that.

Although he knew it was over with Ali, the conflict with Johnny wasn't that simple. He'd have to finish his karate training and meet Johnny at the tournament, completing the battle they'd begun that first day on the beach. What would things be like now if he'd never showed off his hot dog soccer moves to Ali? Different. Very different.

That afternoon Daniel sat at the oars of a rowboat on a lake with Mr. Miyagi. No mention was made of the scene at Mr. Miyagi's on Friday night. It was as if it had never happened. But it had.

"Stop. Stand. Bow," commanded the old man.

Carefully, Daniel lay down the oars and stood, bowing courteously.

"Not bow. *Bow*," said Mr. Miyagi, pointing to the front of the boat. Daniel laughed at the mistake and cautiously stood at the bow, feeling somewhat like George Washington crossing the Delaware.

"Now, make block," Mr. Miyagi ordered. "Up down, side side. Left right. Breathe in, breathe out. Remember breathe most important, Danielsan. Lose control breathe in, breathe out, lose control of whole body. Center of life is breathe."

Daniel nodded and began the blocking and breathing exercises. At first, it was very difficult, but, as with the kicks in the waves at the ocean, he caught the rhythm of the rocking boat in the still water and began to feel secure.

"When am I going to learn to punch?" he asked.

In response, Mr. Miyagi began to rock the boat, breaking Daniel's rhythm and tipping him. Unceremoniously, Daniel landed, shoulder first, in the cold water. When he emerged, sputtering, Mr. Miyagi answered his question.

"When learn keep dry," he said wryly, and helped Daniel climb back into the boat.

"More important than learn punch or block," he continued, handing Daniel a towel, "is to learn balance. Balance is key. When balance good, karate good. Everything good. When balance bad, better fix quick or pack up and go home. Understand?"

"Yeah."

"Then go practice." Daniel returned to the bow. "And no scare fish," Mr. Miyagi admonished him, baiting the hook on his fishing line.

Hundreds of blocks and three fish later, Daniel spoke again, without breaking his tempo.

"You ever get into fights when you were a kid?"

"Lots."

"But it wasn't like the problem I have."

"Why not? Fighting all same."

"Well, for one thing, you knew karate."

"Always someone else know more. No different from now."

"You mean there were times when you were scared to fight?"

"Scared *all* times, Danielsan. Hate fighting."

"But you like karate."

"So?"

"Karate is fighting. That's why you train: to fight."

"That what you think, really?"

Was it? Daniel thought a moment.

"No."

"Why train then?" the old man challenged.

"So I won't have to fight."

Mr. Miyagi smiled broadly, obviously proud of Daniel's growing wisdom.

"Hope for you yet," he complimented. "Come, row."

"Where to?" asked Daniel, obeying.

"Ready to learn punch."

Chapter
Twenty-three

"ONE inch," said Mr. Miyagi, standing on the new deck of his house. "Secret of punch is to make whole power of body fit into one inch."

"Oh yeah?" said Daniel, laughing at the idea. "Which inch?"

In a split second, Mr. Miyagi's fist came into Daniel's vision, powered by the awesome energy of the old man's body. The fist stopped as suddenly as it had started, a hair's breadth from Daniel's nose. Mr. Miyagi pointed to his first two knuckles.

"This inch."

Daniel understood.

Mr. Miyagi donned a catcher's chest protector with a bull's eye painted in the middle. "Focus target. Make all power go here," he said, tapping his knuckles. "Direct to here." He tapped the red circle. "Now punch."

Hesitantly, Daniel struck at Mr. Miyagi,

but the weak punch had no effect. Annoyed, Mr. Miyagi commanded, "Harder! Focus!"

Daniel tried again, but it was little better.

"What you, some kind of weakling? Now *focus!*"

Again, Daniel failed.

"You are wasting my time! You not listen, you lazy! Now punch hard or go home!"

Hurt and angry, Daniel made a fist to lunge at the old man. Suddenly, he realized he *could* feel the power concentrating in his knuckles.

"Kiaiii!" he yelled and landed the punch on the bull's eye, knocking Mr. Miyagi onto his back. The feeling was wonderful, it was strength, it was energy, and it was, above all, success.

"Hey, hey!" he said, glowing as he watched Mr. Miyagi in the dust. "You look like a turtle. One-Punch LaRusso scores again! What do you think, huh?"

Mr. Miyagi exploded from the dirt, foot trapping Daniel who hit the ground face first. Before he knew what had happened, Mr. Miyagi chopped him on the back of the neck.

"Think you talk too much, Mr. One-Punch. Concentrate too little. Now up — up! You waste time. Tournament around corner."

Sobered, Daniel rose and brushed himself off.

"Why'd you have to remind me?"

The next afternoon, Daniel was back at the beach — this time alone.

With the utmost care, he made his way to the last piling and pulled himself up on its precarious surface. Carefully, between waves, he stood as straight and tall as he could and lifted his right leg into the crane position he'd seen Mr. Miyagi use, in time to greet the oncoming wave. At the last second, he flexed his left leg to jump, but he was too late. The powerful sea grabbed him and pulled him from the piling, slamming him into another one, making a gash in his head. He lost his sense of direction as the water tossed and dragged him mercilessly. He struggled against the clawing grasp of the undertow, barely escaping its pull. Continuously, the waves pushed him to danger while the undertow dragged him to the depths.

It took every ounce of Daniel's strength to overcome the forces of the icy Pacific, but some time later, coughing up salty water, Daniel pulled himself onto the beach, exhausted, spent.

It was then, semiconscious, that Daniel remembered Mr. Miyagi's words:

"First learn stand, then learn fly. Nature's rules, Danielsan, not mine."

How long, he wondered, lying half in and half out of the water, still unable to move. How long before he could stand?

Chapter
Twenty-four

Sixteen. Sixteen at last!

Daniel entered Mr. Miyagi's cabin that night to find a traditional American birthday party, with some Japanese flavor, in progress. He was the guest of honor, of course, Mr. Miyagi the host, and the karate practice dummy, whom they'd dubbed Hashimoto, the only other invited guest.

Mr. Miyagi, wearing a pointed, crepe-papered hat, entered, singing and carrying a birthday cake whose candles were the only illumination in the room.

"Make wish," he ordered.

That was easy. Making it come true would be the hard part, thought Daniel, recalling Ali's beautiful smile. He blew out all the candles.

When Mr. Miyagi lit the gas lantern, Daniel found a package in front of him. He opened it as Mr. Miyagi cut and served the cake.

"So, how spend birthday?"

"Got my driver's license."

"Congratulations, Danielsan. Now you don't need learn to fly. You can drive," he teased.

Daniel smiled and then lifted the lid from the box. It was a brand new gi. On the back of the jacket a bonsai tree was embroidered and above it were some Japanese characters. "Miyagi-do Karate," Mr. Miyagi read. Daniel was stunned.

He tried the jacket on immediately. It fit perfectly.

"Oh, man, thanks, Mr. Miyagi. You, too, Mr. Hashimoto. It's great!" He stood and tried some blocks and kicks. Somehow, the jacket made it all feel so much more like the real thing. Then, he remembered that it *was* the real thing — that the tournament was the next day. Deflated, he sat down and began to eat the cake.

"You think I have a chance?"

"Not important what Miyagi think. Miyagi not fighting."

"I don't feel like I know much stuff."

"Feeling correct."

"Boy, you sure know how to make a guy feel good," said Daniel, laughing in spite of the gloomy outlook.

Mr. Miyagi smiled and bowed.

"Trust quality, not quantity, Danielsan."

Daniel wanted to change the subject. "Look," he said, displaying his brand new driver's license.

Mr. Miyagi dutifully admired it, but his eye was caught by something else in Daniel's wallet — a picture of Daniel and Ali taken at the arcade that night so long ago.

"Didn't know you had sweetheart," he said, pulling the picture out to inspect it.

"I don't."

"Look nice together," Mr. Miyagi said, analytically. "Different, but same."

"Nah. Different, but different," said Daniel, taking off the jacket.

"Where you going? Can't leave without Miyagi's present."

"Oh, hey, Mr. Miyagi, you really have given me enough —"

"No lip," Mr. Miyagi chided, walking to the door. "Just come."

Daniel followed him out the door and they stood looking at the vintage automobiles.

"Choose," he said, gesturing toward the cars. Daniel was awestruck. Could he *really* mean —

"Oh, no, no, I can't. I *couldn't* —"

"Hurt old man's feelings, Danielsan."

Well, yes, he *could* choose. Unhesitatingly, Daniel walked to the yellow Chevrolet convertible, opened the door, and climbed in, enjoying, once again, the regal feeling of being so far above the ground.

With a start, Daniel saw that the keys

were in the ignition, that the key chain was Mr. Miyagi's dog tags. He'd known what car Daniel would choose. Daniel was so overcome, he couldn't speak.

"Remember, license no replace eyes and ears," Mr. Miyagi warned him, helping Daniel to recover, but at that moment, Daniel remembered the tournament and his spirit broke.

"I'm scared," he confessed.

"Understand. Should be. Remember lesson of balance, yes?"

"Yes."

"Not just lesson for karate, Danielsan. Lesson for whole life. Whole life, if you balance, everything you do will be better. Karate, too." Mr. Miyagi handed Daniel the picture of him and Ali. "Understand?"

Daniel nodded, smiling.

"Thanks for everything, Mr. Miyagi. You are the best friend I ever knew."

"You pretty okay, too, Danielsan," said Mr. Miyagi, smiling. "Now, go," he urged. "Go!"

Daniel turned the key and glowed at the purr of the engine. He shifted into reverse, released the emergency brake, and let out the clutch.

"Banzai!" called Mr. Miyagi.

"*Banzai!*" Daniel answered happily.

Chapter
Twenty-five

"ALI!" Daniel called out across the parking lot at the arcade, but either she couldn't hear him, or she wouldn't. She disappeared into the arcade with two friends. Quickly, Daniel parked the convertible and followed her inside.

Within a few minutes, his eyes were adjusted to the darkness punctuated by flashing neon lights. He wandered along the aisles, looking for Ali. When he saw her and her friends, they were at the shooting gallery. He ran over and stood between her and the target.

"Don't shoot! Can we talk?"

Ali was cold.

"I have nothing to say." Well, he hadn't expected a red carpet, considering their last meeting. He tried to joke as she began to walk away.

"Don't leave me, I'm wounded."

Ali ignored him, but her friend answered for her.

"Good. Maybe you'll die." The girls moved to other arcade games. Daniel followed and spoke again to Ali.

"Look, I just want to apologize."

"Fine. You apologized."

This was tougher than he had expected.

"I got my license."

"Happy birthday," she said dully. It struck him as ironic that he didn't seem to be able to accomplish the one thing that would now make it a completely happy birthday. He began to lose his resolve and his balance.

"What's with you?" he challenged.

"What do you expect? Cartwheels?"

"No," he answered. "Just a little courtesy. But I guess that's only reserved for people with a Porsche or a Mercedes."

His balance was gone.

Ali walked away, but Daniel wasn't finished.

"What's the matter? Truth hurt?" he blurted.

"You really think that's it, don't you?"

"I *know* that's it."

"Well, you're wrong."

"I *bet.*"

"I don't go out with someone because of where he lives or if he has a car."

"So why did you go out with me?"

"I thought, maybe, you and me — well, we're different."

"That's the point, isn't it? We *are* different. I'm from Reseda and you're from the Hills."

"That's not what I meant."

"Why don't you just admit that you can't handle the situation?"

"*I* can handle it fine, Daniel," she said. "*You* can't."

That hurt. It hurt badly because it was true. It hurt too much to admit, so he lashed out at her.

"You don't know what you're talking about!"

Ali turned and walked away, tears welling up in her eyes. Daniel watched, dismayed that things had gotten this bad for them. His thoughts were interrupted by Ali's friend.

"What makes you so insensitive?" she said, accusingly. "She's never been anything but nice to you."

"Oh, yeah," he responded. "She was so nice she even let me be her tool to make what's-his-name jealous."

"She doesn't even *like* Johnny!"

"I never could have guessed that from the way their faces were stuck together at the country club."

"Oh, that's right. You were so eager to get out that you didn't stick around for the exciting conclusion."

"Yeah, what was that?"

"Her right hook. You think she sprained her wrist polishing her nails?"

"She hit him?"

"That's an understatement."

"So why didn't she say something to me?"

"She shouldn't have to, should she?" She turned and walked away, leaving Daniel alone with his shame.

He wasted no more time. He ran out of the arcade, looking for Ali. She tried to avoid him, but her defenses were weak.

"I'm a jerk," he said, disarmingly and truthfully.

"Yeah, you are," she confirmed, smiling and nodding.

"Can you forgive a jerk?" He held his arms out invitingly. For one awful moment, she stood there, looking at him and not moving. Then Ali walked to him and let him envelop her.

"Sure," she said. They hugged warmly, both very relieved.

"Hey, I almost forgot, Ali, I want to show you something," he said, leading her over to the car.

"How do you like it?"

"This is yours?" she asked, excited. Daniel nodded and displayed the keys.

"Oh, it's wonderful. Beautiful. It's the neatest car I've ever seen."

"You want to drive?"

"Me? Wow!" She kissed him on the cheek and ran to the driver's seat. They both climbed in for a drive.

Much later, they pulled up in front of Ali's house. Ali combed her windblown hair and asked, unnecessarily, "How do I look?"

"Really beautiful." He put his arm up around her shoulder and wiped a smudge from her forehead, pleased with the calm of the moment. He was uncertain about the future — their future and his. After all, there was the tournament in the morning, but at that instant, he knew he was where he wanted to be.

"I'm in the karate tournament tomorrow."

"I know."

"So I guess you're already invited."

Ali nodded, and Daniel's hopes sank.

"But I haven't accepted," said Ali. "However, I *have* decided to accept the very *next* invitation I get," she said impishly, smiling.

"Will you be my guest?"

"I thought you'd never ask."

"I'll probably get killed in the first match."

Ali's eyes twinkled.

"So we'll leave early."

What a girl, he thought, reaching to hold her warmly. Softly, they kissed good-night.

Chapter
Twenty-six

"KIAIIIIII!"

The cry echoed through the competition hall, which throbbed with excitement as Daniel, Ali, and Mr. Miyagi entered the next day.

Hundreds of kids filled the arena, milling around, warming up, and practicing. They all looked confident and capable. That wasn't how Daniel felt. What he felt was anxious and scared. He figured that's how he'd feel all day long, too.

"What's your belt, LaRusso?" the man at the registration desk asked, looking at Daniel's new white belt. Daniel wanted to answer, "J.C. Penny, $3.98," but Mr. Miyagi responded with a question:

"Why need rank?"

"Open divisions are only for brown belt and above." Daniel's heart sank.

"Boy is black belt," Mr. Miyagi answered,

surprising Daniel. The registrar filled in the form and handed Mr. Miyagi the completed papers.

"Better hustle. They're starting soon."

Together, the three of them walked toward the rings in the cavernous competition hall. Daniel was a little envious of the brown and black belts he saw on the boys around him, but he was comforted by the knowledge that at least he didn't need a rope to hold up his pants.

They stopped for a moment for Mr. Miyagi to consult the papers and to become oriented in the hall. With the papers in one hand, Mr. Miyagi held out a black belt to Daniel with the other.

"Where'd you get this?" Daniel asked, frankly thrilled as he put it on.

"Buddha provide," he answered enigmatically. "Draw ring three. Come," he said, pointing to the left. As they walked back, Daniel noticed one of the officials, gi flapping open, looking furiously for something — obviously his belt. Buddha, thought Daniel, laughing to himself, must be a 70-year-old pickpocket!

Just then, the public address system announced the arrival of the Cobra Kai. Daniel stopped, with the rest of the milling crowd, to watch them make their entrance. They were running in double-time military style, chanting the familiar, chilling cadence. Johnny led them.

"What do we study?"

"THE WAY OF THE FIST!"

"What is that way?"

"STRIKE FIRST! STRIKE HARD!"

Well, today was the day, thought Daniel. He would be testing the Way of the Fist against the Way of Miyagi. Daniel felt his anxiety fade. He realized that no matter what happened, he was prepared to do his best. He would gain and keep his self-respect whether he won or lost. Also, he knew this was a much better arena to test his abilities than against a chain-link fence behind the school yard.

He'd come a long way in a few months. He thought of that fateful — and very phony — karate kick he'd made at the door on the day he arrived, and the lies that had followed. In a way, he was grateful to his lies because, without them, he never would have gotten to this point — probably never would have gotten to know Mr. Miyagi and never would have become so close to Ali. But he'd also learned that he didn't have to lie. Lies upset balance and made life very difficult.

"LaRusso!" Daniel looked up at the referee who was inviting him to step into the ring with a young Goliath named Rufus. Daniel stared at Rufus who was a head taller than himself while the referee reminded them of the rules.

"My word is law. Don't listen and you're

out. Make contact, except in a clash, you're out. Strike the groin, the knees, the throat, the eyes, you're out. Now bow."

They bowed to each other.

"Engarde. Begin."

Rufus opened with an explosive back kick, catching Daniel in the shoulder and lifting him right out of the ring. The referee signalled him to come back.

"Try to keep it in the ring, LaRusso. Continue." Some bystanders laughed.

Daniel realized he would have to keep his attention as focussed on his opponent as his power could be focussed into one square inch. He couldn't afford to let his mind wander.

Rufus charged, throwing a barrage of punches, but none of them landed effectively. They did, however, drive Daniel back to the edge of the ring. The referee snapped at him, "One more warning, LaRusso," he threatened. "Engarde. Continue."

Daniel walked back to the center of the ring, noting as he did that several Cobras stood in the audience, eyeing him smugly. That was enough.

When Rufus charged with a side kick, Daniel sidestepped, mid-blocked, and fired a reverse punch to the spine.

"Point. Punch. LaRusso. Continue."

Rufus charged again, this time with a front punch. Daniel hopped to the side deftly and snapped a roundhouse kick to the boy's stomach. It wasn't a great kick, but it was sufficient to halt Rufus and deflate him.

"Point. Kick. LaRusso. Bow. Winner, LaRusso, Miyagi-do."

The Cobras stared icily. Ali cheered wildly. Mr. Miyagi, never one to show much emotion, simply beamed. One-Punch LaRusso had learned his lesson though. Winning one match was hardly the same as winning the next or beating Johnny. He still had a long way to go in the tournament. Cockiness wouldn't get him there.

In the next hour, he had two more matches, neither as hard as the one with Rufus, though both opponents were tougher than Rufus. The lesson on concentration that Daniel had learned from Rufus was a valuable one.

After the first match, Daniel had watched as his opponent's mother comforted him. Daniel wondered where his mother was, wondered if she would be angry when she found his note about the tournament on the refrigerator. By the end of the second match, that question was answered.

Daniel's opponent charged with a punch. Left, right. Left, right. Breathe in out. Daniel blocked to the inside, then counterpunched.

"Punch. Point. Winner, LaRusso, Miyagi-do."

The boys bowed to the referee. Suddenly, Daniel became aware of a loud clapping and a very familiar voice cheering. He lifted his eyes to meet those of his mother. She was glowing with pride, and ran to him when he stepped out of the ring.

"Oh, Daniel, you were fantastic!" she said, hugging him. "I was so scared when I saw your note that I almost got three speeding tickets getting here, but then I looked at the elimination chart and saw you're winning!"

Daniel smiled grandly, basking in the glory of the admiration of the three people he really cared about — his mother, Ali, and Mr. Miyagi.

Chapter
Twenty-seven

OH, brother, thought Daniel later as he watched Johnny's semi-final match. A flying wheel kick was followed by a counterpunch. A fake snap turned into a roundhouse kick.

"This guy has techniques I can't even spell!" he muttered to Mr. Miyagi who was watching intently and just nodded.

Kreese stood at the side of the ring, watching Johnny's victory silently. His eyes caught Daniel's and held them, and for one awful moment, Daniel was frozen in fear. It was almost with relief that Daniel returned his attention to Johnny, realizing Johnny, not Kreese, would be his opponent. Maybe. First, he had to beat Bobby.

When Johnny's match was over, his own was announced.

"Will Daniel LaRusso of Miyagi-do Karate and Bobby Brown of the Cobra Kai please report."

His mother looked at him, trying to hide her nervousness, but she succeeded only in showing her concern.

"Good luck, hon," she said, squeezing his hand.

"Don't worry, Mom," he reassured her. He thought again of her promise of a Garden of Eden. Only problem was the serpent — Cobra, really. Well, he was doing his best on that score.

He climbed into the ring and did his warm-ups. Bobby stood on the side, deep in conversation with Kreese. Daniel watched them uneasily as they spoke, looking up at him in turns. Johnny stood behind them, apparently upset, while Kreese tapped Bobby's knee.

It occurred to Daniel that Kreese could be instructing Bobby to throw the match to assure a match between himself and Johnny. That was not a flattering thought, but there was nothing he could do except to keep his balance, concentrate all his power into one inch, and fight like crazy.

The referee invited them to the center of the ring.

"Bow. Engarde. Begin."

Bobby's first move was a low front kick. Daniel began his block, realizing too late that the low kick was a fake.

Swisssshhhhh.

Bobby's wheel kick whistled an inch from Daniel's ear.

"Point. Brown. Engarde. Continue."

If Bobby was throwing the match, that was a funny way to start.

Daniel and Bobby circled, each looking for an opportunity to strike. Bobby's eyes flicked to Kreese at ringside and Daniel took advantage of the lapse in concentration, lunging with an undeflected punch.

"Point. LaRusso. One, one. Engarde."

Bobby stood still, his eyes locked with Kreese's. Daniel couldn't understand what was happening as he observed a battle of wills between Bobby and Kreese.

"Brown!" the referee snapped. "Engarde!"

Bobby put his hands up, his face resigned. Once again, his eyes shifted to Kreese, then back to Daniel.

"Continue," said the referee.

Suddenly, it was clear to Daniel what was going on and he was helpless to stop it. Kreese hadn't told Bobby to throw the match. He'd told him to take Daniel out — for good!

Bobby sprang high into the air and began to throw a flying kick. Instinctively, Daniel lifted his hands to deflect the blow, but instead of kicking out, Bobby dropped and pushed the blade of his foot into Daniel's unprotected knee.

The sickening *crack* could be heard throughout the arena.

Daniel collapsed and grabbed his knee, feeling the searing pain shoot through his joint. He couldn't have imagined pain like that before he felt it. Tears welled in his eyes and he howled in agony.

It seemed like everything happened in slow motion then. Mr. Miyagi came to him. His mother and Ali, too. Then a stretcher. Bobby stood by his side.

"I'm sorry. I'm sorry. I couldn't —" he was stopped by the referee.

"Bobby Brown of the Cobra Kai will be disqualified for excessive and deliberate contact and prohibited from competing in all further competitions sanctioned by this organization. The winner: Daniel LaRusso."

Daniel barely registered this information. From the stretcher, he watched Bobby exit the ring to catcalls from the audience. Bobby stopped just long enough to untie and discard his belt at Kreese's feet and walk out, shattered.

The Cobra, it seemed, could be poisoned by its own venom.

Chapter
Twenty-eight

DANIEL'S mother held his hand while the doctor examined his throbbing knee. Outside the locker room, in the competition ring, Daniel could hear the crowd applaud a demonstration match. Now, he wondered, would they have a chance to applaud the Championship Match, too, or would Johnny win by default?

The shake of the doctor's head seemed to answer that question. Then he spoke. "I'm sorry. I'll inform the judges."

Daniel's mother squeezed his hand, trying to comfort him.

"I couldn't be prouder of you," she said, showing she understood that the greater pain for Daniel was not being able to finish.

"I didn't have a chance anyway."

"That's not true," said Ali, loyally.

"Don't you think it's time for a little reality here?"

"I'm not kidding. I've seen a lot of these things and I think you had a shot."

"Well, we'll never know, will we?" he retorted cynically.

Mr. Miyagi said nothing, but slowly, he began to rub his hands together, in circles. With each turn, they went faster and faster until it seemed they were smoking with the speed. He walked to Daniel and stood by his aching knee. With calm assurance, he reached for Daniel's leg.

Ten minutes later, the crowd listened to the tournament official as he was about to hand the trophy to Johnny. Daniel could hear it from the door of the locker room.

"This young man has shown us some very fine karate today, folks. And the fact that his final opponent has been disabled takes nothing away from the skill young John Lawrence has mastered."

The crowd applauded, and the official continued.

Suddenly, there was a ripple in the crowd.

"Wait a minute!" cried Ali, running from the locker room. The crowd turned to watch.

First came Ali, then Daniel, then his mother and Mr. Miyagi. Daniel didn't know why or how he could walk on that knee, but he could. Somehow, some way, his knee was working. He could flex it, straighten it, rotate it, and move the calf from side to side. He couldn't feel very much with the numbed joint, but he suspected that was for the best.

The standing crowd parted to make a path for them, walking toward the ring. An astonished Kreese was the first of the three in the ring to see him. The fury in his face made the other two look up as well. Johnny's face was almost blank. Daniel wondered for an instant if there was a slight flicker of relief in those stony eyes, but rejected the thought. Only the official showed unmasked joy.

"Look at this young man, folks! Let's give him a hand." Then, addressing Daniel, "How's that leg, son?"

In answer, Daniel threw two kicks, his eyes frozen to Johnny's.

The official patted him on the back and spoke to the crowd again.

"Isn't that just exactly what this is all about, folks?" The crowd clapped in appreciation, but Daniel hardly heard them at all.

"All right now, folks," boomed the announcer over the public address system. "Here is the big event. The title match to determine victor and champion of the All Valley Under 18 Championship. Daniel LaRusso, Miyagi-do Karate versus John Lawrence of the Cobra Kai."

Johnny and Daniel met at center ring.

"You know the rules, boys. Three points wins. Let's give these people a championship match they won't forget."

That's just what Daniel intended to do. The look in Johnny's eyes confirmed his agreement on that point.

"Bow. Engarde. Begin."

Johnny opened with a flurry of punches and kicks, driving Daniel back. Then Johnny switched to a wheel kick, which Daniel evaded by ducking and countered with a strong reverse punch to the stomach.

"Point. LaRusso. Continue."

The crowd was still and silent — almost as if they feared to break the boys' concentration. Daniel and Johnny circled, each looking for a point of attack, each oblivious to the rest of the world.

Suddenly, Johnny lashed out with a backhand slap, followed immediately by a strong side kick. While Johnny's leg reached for Daniel, Daniel dropped onto the mat, and, sitting, shot his legs around on either side of Johnny's support leg. Before Johnny could even get his other foot to the floor, Daniel twisted his legs around Johnny's ankle and brought his opponent crashing to the mat. Swiftly, Daniel scrambled to his knees and delivered a chop to Johnny's neck.

"Point. LaRusso."

The crowd burst into applause, stunned by Daniel's lightning reflexes and sure technique. For a brief moment, Daniel listened to the appreciative shouts and clapping. He enjoyed it. He noticed a look of surprise mixed with admiration from Johnny.

In a way, it didn't matter to Daniel who

won the match now. Daniel had won the crowd's respect; he'd won Johnny's respect; most important, however, he'd won his own self-respect. Just as Mr. Miyagi had promised, he couldn't lose.

"Engarde. Continue," said the referee.

Johnny exploded with a full-powered foot sweep, which caught Daniel just below his bad knee. Daniel reeled in pain, and spun off balance, right into Johnny's punch to his back.

"Point. Lawrence."

The Cobra Kai contingent began to cheer for their hero. They cheered even more loudly when they watched Daniel limp back to the center of the ring.

"Engarde. Continue."

Again, Johnny threw a sweep at Daniel. Daniel swirled right into Johnny's roundhouse kick to the head. It caught him full in the mouth, splitting Daniel's lip, and knocking him to the mat. He pulled himself up slowly, wiping the blood with his sleeve. The referee spoke.

"Clash. No contact. Point. Lawrence."

The boys returned to the center of the ring.

"Two—two. Match point. Engarde. Continue."

Johnny flexed his knees, ready to attack with a lethal foot sweep once again, ready to finish his limping opponent once and for all. But Daniel was prepared to counter offensively.

He was, in fact, ready to fly. And he knew it.

As Johnny began his circle, Daniel raised his bad leg up and tucked it close to his body. He lifted his hands in front of him in perfect imitation of Mr. Miyagi's crane. Quickly, he caught his teacher's eyes and saw a small smile form on the old man's lips, a glow in his eyes.

Johnny seemed confused and hesitated. The referee interrupted.

"Continue."

Johnny still stared, uncertain what was coming and how to attack. He was brought up sharply, however, by Kreese's gravelly shout —

"Finish him!"

Johnny took a deep breath and lunged. Too late.

With incredible precision, Daniel lifted his body straight up into the air and using every remaining ounce of strength, his good leg shot out, caught Johnny on the jaw and catapulted him onto the mat.

Daniel landed amid shouts of awe and admiration from the crowd and then his leg collapsed, dropping him to the mat as well. As he pulled himself up, he watched Kreese stalking furiously out of the competition hall, looking like nothing so much as a spoiled child.

Finally, Daniel stood next to Johnny. They bowed. Their eyes met in genuine respect while Johnny took the trophy out of the referee's hands and gave it to Daniel.

"Good match," Johnny said sincerely. Daniel smiled and thanked him.

The referee raised Daniel's arm in victory. "Point. Flying kick. LaRusso. Winner."

What sweet words those were!

Chapter
Twenty-nine

A HALF hour later, Daniel, his mother, Ali, and Mr. Miyagi walked happily from the nearly empty competition hall.

"Lobsters are on me," Daniel's mother announced. "I'm going to go set up."

She turned to leave, but then stopped, returning to Daniel.

"You're marvelous," she said, kissing him. He was a little embarrassed, but nobody else seemed to care, so he simply smiled. Then his mother turned to Mr. Miyagi and kissed him as well.

"You're marvelous, too," she said.

With a start, she realized she might have offended him, and asked, blushing, "Oh. Is that an insult?"

Mr. Miyagi bowed ceremoniously, "At my age, compliment."

They all laughed and Lucille ran to her

car. "Don't be long," she called. Ali took Daniel's hand.

As they rounded the building, they could see Kreese talking to Johnny. In fact, Kreese held him by the shirt and was snarling with fury.

"I had him crippled for you and you still couldn't beat him!"

"It wasn't my fault," Johnny answered.

"You implying it was *mine*?"

From the side, Mr. Miyagi spoke.

"Why you no pick on someone your own size?"

"Mind your own business, old man."

"Who you calling old man, monkey face?"

Kreese met the challenge by shoving Johnny aside like a rag doll. The vicious sensei rushed Mr. Miyagi with a lunge, punching at his face. With a sinking heart, Daniel realized there was no referee here, nobody to keep it clean.

Kreese's fist was fast, but not fast enough. Mr. Miyagi calmly sidestepped the punch and it landed on the windshield of the car behind him, creating a spider web pattern around Kreese's bruised fist. Enraged, Kreese lunged again. This time, Mr. Miyagi did not sidestep. At the last possible moment, he raised his hand, palm out, and intercepted Kreese's fist. Kreese stopped dead in his tracks. A cold smile seemed to touch the corners of Mr. Miyagi's mouth as he slowly applied pressure to Kreese's fist, forcing him to the ground.

Kreese was on his knees, held frozen by Mr. Miyagi's left hand. Daniel was proud of his teacher and of the evident awe Kreese's students showed for Mr. Miyagi.

Then, to Daniel's horror, Mr. Miyagi brought back his powerful right hand, cocked for action, and spoke. It was Mr. Miyagi's voice, but these were not his words.

"Mercy is for the weak. We do not train to be merciful. A man faces you. He is the enemy. An enemy deserves no mercy."

Daniel looked at Mr. Miyagi in surprise, but the old man's face was a mask of vengeance.

No. This could *not* be Mr. Miyagi. This was not the man who had taught him self-respect. No. Daniel could not believe what he was seeing.

He glanced at the Cobra Kai students, frightened at the strength of the old man's hatred, sure of the revenge it would serve on their sensei. Then Daniel looked at Kreese, the man of ice, melted by fear.

Mr. Miyagi's eyes flashed. His cocked hand sailed through the air, whistling toward Kreese's unprotected head.

Daniel closed his eyes. Then looked.

The chop had stopped with the same power that propelled it, less than an inch from Kreese's nose. A minute passed. Then, Mr. Miyagi's forefinger flicked out and nubbed Kreese's nose in the lowest form of insult.

Briefly, Mr. Miyagi looked to Daniel, and winked. A feeling of relief rushed through Daniel as he watched him step away from Kreese. Daniel ran to Mr. Miyagi, his friend, his teacher, and embraced him, filled with pride and happiness. With his other hand, he reached for Ali and together, the three of them walked to the Chevy convertible.

Daniel paused to look over his shoulder at the Cobra Kai. One by one, he saw the students take off their belts and drop them in front of the still kneeling Kreese. One by one, they walked away from him, away from the way of the fist. At last, they were learning the lesson of balance, the true way of karate.

Daniel turned around again, admiring the gleaming trophy that Ali carried.

How can I go wrong, he thought, with a terrific man like Mr. Miyagi for a friend, the most beautiful magician in the world for a girl friend, and a mother who will spring for lobsters everytime I win the All Valley Under 18 Karate Championship.

A guy could really turn on to a Garden of Eden like this.

point

Other books you will enjoy, about real kids like you!

- ☐ 40708-2 **Acts of Love** Maureen Daly
- ☐ 40545-4 **A Band of Angels** Julian F. Thompson
- ☐ 41289-2 **The Changeover: A Supernatural Romance** Margaret Mahy
- ☐ 40251-X **Don't Care High** Gordon Korman
- ☐ 40969-7 **How Do You Lose Those Ninth Grade Blues?** Barthe DeClements
- ☐ 40935-2 **Last Dance** Caroline B. Cooney
- ☐ 40548-9 **A Royal Pain** Ellen Conford
- ☐ 41115-2 **Seventeen and In-Between** Barthe DeClements
- ☐ 33254-6 **Three Sisters** Norma Fox Mazer
- ☐ 40832-1 **Twisted** R.L. Stine
- ☐ 40383-4 **When the Phone Rang** Harry Mazer
- ☐ 40205-6 **Yearbook** Melissa Davis

Available wherever you buy books... or use the coupon below. $2.50 each

---

Scholastic Inc.
P.O. Box 7502, 2932 East McCarty Street, Jefferson City, MO 65102

Please send me the books I have checked above. I am enclosing $ _____
(please add $1.00 to cover shipping and handling). Send check or money order—
no cash or C.O.D.'s please.

Name_____

Address_____

City_____State/Zip_____

Please allow four to six weeks for delivery. Offer good in U.S.A. only. Sorry, mail order not
available to residents of Canada. Prices subject to change.   PNT987